SECOND
EDITION

www.adipintotheforbidden.com

Dedication

I want to dedicate this book to my parents for starters. They have stood by me through hell and back. I love you Mom and Dad. I also want to dedicate this book to my daughters Lejla aka Lejlaboo and Amelija aka Mills Chunky Mama. We are growing up in a world where we still are told what can and cannot do. Where limits are placed on our persons. I want them to know that despite popular belief, the sky is not the limit. There is a whole Universe to explore.

Zahara .

Table of Contents

Excerpt

Her alter ego Penny awakens as she turns around and sees Braxton writing his name on a tall woman's dance card. He leaned down and kissed her on the cheek. Eva was lost in thought, thinking this was the woman who interrupted what could have been the best night of her life. *It still can be*, Penny rants at her. Eva knew she should not be here at this ball staring intently like a brazen she-devil at Braxton. What was the alternative? He was the most beautiful man she had ever seen. He was tall, broad shouldered, with unique silver eyes, and dark chestnut hair.

Tonight, he wore his hair slicked back just long enough to be tied back at his neck. Braxton looked nothing short of regal. Prince Harry, she thought. He completed his look with a tailored long tail black suit with a matching silver waistband matching the allure of his prince charming vibes. Eva felt herself warm underneath her mask as she was mentally stripping his clothes off of his body. Suddenly he looked up, locked eyes with her, and started in Eva's direction. She quickly glanced down, ashamed of where her thoughts were going.

"Excuse me Miss…" she was struck dumbly.

"E..va.." She replied, staggering her words a little bit like a drunkard on the street. The light of recognition lit his silver eyes. "Miss Eva, I have never seen you at one of these functions before. Granted, it is always a masked affair, so I am happy to make your acquaintance."

"Mr. Carter, there are over two hundred people here. I am sure you do not see every one of them."

Darn it! She thought.

Now he knows she was staring at him and knew who he was BY LAST NAME.

Anymore lame and I'll be needing a crutch. Eva wanted to melt, his gaze seemed to penetrate into her. Why does she always have to be awkward and rhetorical? It's a ridiculous combination. He tipped his head back and laughed, showing off a perfect set of pearly white teeth. She was in trouble.

Chapter One:

Evangeline

Thursday April 5, 2012

Evangeline, also known as Eva, was tucked nicely into her twin-size bed in her shared apartment. This was the day after the big party her roommate Susan hosted at a popular club near campus. Nothing to celebrate really other than a few weeks left of the semester. Her alarm clock rang with such ferocity she was sure she was in mid battle. At least that is how her dreaming-self interpreted it, quite literally as a matter of fact. Evangeline woke groggy unwilling to put forth the required energy to set the snooze or shut off the alarm. It felt like she just went to sleep. After what seemed like an hour of drifting in and out of sleep from the alarm, she woke up and read the time on the clock at 6:58 AM. *Oh, crap!* It was her first thought as she jumped exuberantly out of bed. The last thing she needed was to be late and have to hear about it from her boss.

"Shit! Shit! Shit! I'm going to be late for work." With how unruly her hair was to how lazily she perused in the morning she needed at least an hour and a half.

Evangeline worked with a cleaning agency for the last three years of her college life. Granted it was part time, but the pay was better than the starting pay at most places. It allowed her to continue going to college and save money. In the last two years she was placed at the Carter's family estate. Unlike other families she had worked for, the home was almost always completely empty except for the cleaning staff. *Oh, really, and what about the heir of the estate...forgot him so soon huh.* That was Penny, Eva's alter ego that always seemed to come out and encourage poor behavior at all times. As usual, Eva was daydreaming and having full dialogs with her inner self and lost track of time.

Whelp there is another ten minutes gone, sigh.

At that last thought she jumped up and raced towards her bathroom. With no time to comb through her lion's mane, she tied her hair under a bandana and placed her cap onto her suffering hair, screaming for a little TLC.

Evangeline was not very tall, only two inches of being a certified little person. One could never see her womanly curves, as she dressed at all times in complete modesty. She looked at her doe-y brown eyes that were too big for her face, full lips that she hated one hundred percent of the time and thick manly eyebrows. Finally deciding she was dressed properly, she walked through the living room to grab the keys to her roommates Cadillac CTS-V. Normally she would take the bus but as time is of the essence, she needed to leave ASAP, besides she thought Susan never minds when she takes the car to work. Not that she will be up by the time her shift ends.

Eva stopped by Rogers Coffee House on the way to her job to grab a quick shot of Espresso. "Good Morning Eva, same as usual?"

"Hey there Mr. Roger, how are the grandkids? And today let's do a double shot of espresso, running behind and need a quick energy boost if I am to get through the day, you know."

Mr. Roger was the neighborhood's grandfather. When she lived in an orphanage, he always came every Friday to drop donuts and cider for all the kids. As Eva grew up, she would help pass out the goodies to all the younger orphans and assist with the cleanup, which is how Mr. and Mrs. Rogers became a big part of her life.

"The Grands are good, very busy. You know Martha doesn't even come to the shop much anymore now that Sabrina gave us another youngin.' Now you make sure you get some rest. No old lady like you should be drinking Espresso that's for us young folks. You get some rest ya hear" He said with a wink.

"OK! I promise." She said kissing him on the cheek and waving goodbye. Mr. and Mrs. Rogers had a quaint little coffee house two blocks from her apartment. It was very homey and decorated with trinkets from their native land and culture. Barbados. The coffee was imported from their family farm and was the best in town. *Heck, probably the state*, she thought.

Eva pulled up at exactly 7:58 am. Pulling her badge out and putting it on the sensor so the gates leading to the forbidden fruit will take her up the drive to her workplace. The mansion resembled the chateau look of the Biltmore Mansion in North Carolina. Not comparable in size but style absolutely.

Thank God I only have to clean two studies and two libraries. If there were more to do, I would never have a chance to finish my degree or live. But! Her alter ego suggested, *you wouldn't be able to feed your thirst for first edition books or see our lover.*

Had it not been for her therapist, she would swear she was going crazy with all the conversing she does in her head. Eva made her way to the side entrances that took her directly to the Service Entrance. This is where she gets her supplies for the day.

This also happens to be where many of the service employees gather to break and gossip. Which is exactly what Gretchen was doing. Eva overheard her telling Jerry that Braxton was caught up in another scandal. Apparently, he was seen with a Mrs. emphasizing the MRS and leaving a certain four seasons. *Blah, Blah, Blah,* she thought as she hurried from the room. Normally she could take a little eavesdropping but today she was just in a sour mood and Braxton Carter was the last name she wanted to hear. Eva made an unwritten rule. *Never befriend anyone that works with her.* * Upon other Dos and Don'ts according to Human Resource.

1.) Don't Steal

2.) Do your work and only your work. And

3.) Do not involve yourself in family affairs be invisible. All those rules were fine with her, she made it her business to be invisible. Especially with Braxton in close proximity.

The guy was too intoxicating for his own good. She was nearing the first library and heard hushed tones inside, so she had to forgo her normal routine, so she was not spotted. Well, almost.

"You there, come here for a moment, will you?" Melony was the stepmother.

"Hello Mrs. Carter, did you need something?" Eva was on high alert, the family has never in almost three years said a word to her, let alone demanded her attention.

"Yes, you will do just fine." Mrs. Carter was sizing Eva up and down almost as if checking for imperfection under a scope.

"You will be here in two weeks' time, we are having a going away party of sorts and we need trusted people. I trust you will be discreet." Before Eva could talk herself out of it, Mrs. Carter gave her a nice boon.

"Of course, this will be separate from your wages, say $3,000 for your help?" While Eva did not object, Mrs. Carter took it as an agreement.

"Great, go now to Jeffrey so he can add your name to the list and explain what is expected." Eva just nodded her head and went to the Service area and sought out Jeffrey.

Not that she would object to an extra three grand, which was almost a quarter of what she managed to save in three years.

She was just hoping this wasn't some freaky cult party. *Oh, but what if it was Penny who came out with a cigar in hand blowing O's.*

"Excuse me Jeffrey, Mrs. Carter sent me to find you in regards to an event they are hosting…"

Jeffrey cut her off with a snap of his fingers. "Not now little one, not here follow me."

Eva not only wished she had not run into Mrs. Carter but was hoping this was not some sacrificial gathering. Surely, she would make like a shooting star and leave. Nevertheless, her curiosity won, and she followed him into a private office. He did not speak for a few moments. "Our employers are hosting an intimate house party with big wigs." He stopped.

"No, you do not need to know who will be here, your job will be to make sure the guests are settled and to keep one guest in particular occupied."

"Now wait a minute, I am not the woman who will be giving favors to any man."

Jeffrey smiled. "Yes, you will do just fine."

"So, I am told." Eva rolled her eyes.

"Do not worry, this is nothing sexual at all, in fact your job will be a companion to Lady Scarlet." This piqued her interest a little.

"During the festivities you will show her the grounds and ensure she is not lacking in attention."

"But why?"

"That dearie is not important, if you can pull this off you will likely be favored by the family."

Again Eva said, "But why me?"

"To answer in short, Mrs. Carter knows everything about the people in her employ and you are a literature major correct?"

"Yes." Eva said quizzically.

"Well, there you have it, you know will be a perfect match for the dear Lady Scarlet, now go ahead and finish up for the day, there will be a package in your car for you with further instructions." He shooed Eva out of the room and resumed picking invisible lint from his perfectly tailored coat. For Eva, if this was just as simple as talking about literature then it could not be so bad. She sped through her duties wiping, dusting, vacuuming, and mopping in record time. As she made her way to her final room, she overheard yet again Gretchen talking about Braxton and his latest scandal. That made her clean with such vigor and anger. It seemed like everyone wanted to discuss Braxton and his nasty ways.

Don't forget they also talk about how sexy he is.

She blushed cherry at her inward thought. This library she always saved last was her favorite. Covered from ceiling to floor with leather bound books in first edition. This particular room looked as if it had never been used since the mansion was built over one hundred years ago. It was all masculine in walnuts and dark cherry woods. Accompanied by a massive six-foot solid wooden desk and two chocolate leather sofas. As usual with time to spare, she sat on the Persian rug and delved into Jane Austen's classic novel Emma. This coincidently reminded Eva of how Susan always tried to set her up with men. Lost in the novel, Eva did not hear the abrupt entrance of the one and only Braxton. She crept slowly to the corner of the massive room trying to make herself invisible. He entered on the phone yelling. "How the hell did they come to that conclusion, four season my ass!" Whoever was on the receiving end she could almost hear the shakiness in their voice.

"Yes well that is what I paid you for so I do not have to deal with this. Figure it out before my father gets wind of this, you know what, just fix it Jay or you're fired." Eva cowered closer to the corner clutching the book, not wanting to move or breathe. Suddenly he sank down in the oversized chair that he seemed to fill nicely

Chapter Two:

Braxton

Braxton paced back and forth in front of the window oblivious to anything going on around him. By now he should have been used to the false news attacking his character. He was sure this was done intentionally by someone on his father's board. With his father almost in retirement and many board members pitching themselves as candidates, somehow this feels like a takeover one in which he will make sure to stop. Braxton stopped suddenly, smelling the most fragrant aroma like a mix of cherries and roses intertwined. He looked around and that is when he saw he was not alone. He walked over to one of the cleaning personnel, and she had a book in her hand. "You've been here the whole time?" She nodded.

"I trust that you will be discreet." The young woman started blushing profusely. Her scent wafted into his nose. He had never seen her here before, granted he doesn't make a point to become acquaintances with people in his employ besides

Nathan. She almost looked scared as he towered over her with his height.

Grabbing the book from her hands, none too softly, he asked, "Do you normally sit and read while I pay you?" She began to shrink inward, and he felt bad about the tone of his voice. That was until the next words left her mouth. Chin held high, the young woman said, "And here I presumed I was being paid by your father. I'll be sure to never touch another book unless I am cleaning it."

With that she turned and left leaving her scent behind and a whisper of words. *What an ass.* Braxton chuckles to himself at her audacity and leaves to meet Nathan to go over some planning. Apparently, his parents were hosting a house party that he must attend that involved many donors for their company.

Chapter Three:

Evangeline

Eva left to go home, excited to see what was in the package that was left by Mrs. Carter. She was still a little confused as to why they had chosen her for this task. If she believed what they said then the only thing that made sense was that she was a loyal employee and whatever they were going to be doing was either highly secretive or super illegal. She hoped for the former. When she returned home she found Susan on the iPad looking earnestly as if trying to find the secret map to Atlantis. Sue had the same look in her eyes and Eva hoped that her friend did not get doped again.

"Hey Sue! How did it go the other night with Mr. Rich IV?" That was their code name for the many rich men that Sue seemed to attract. Sue jumped up from the swivel chair beaming excitedly, "Oh Eva, it was great! We left his club and went to his penthouse, it was so romantic. And he was just the right size you know!" She said while holding her hands out, measuring an invisible penis. Eva looked at her stupidly. Not only did she not "know," she did not want to either. Eva walked to the kitchen grabbing two organic lemonades from the refrigerator. Handing one to Sue, while silently acknowledging this was her best friend's pattern. Find out what she seems to like preferably a rich guy, hook up, go on a few dates, and BOOM he is married.

"Well, I am glad that you enjoyed yourself, I on the other hand woke up late two days in a row, and thankfully I did not drink too much. Otherwise, I would be out of a job with a hangover."

"Eva you are such a prude! That guy Bill, Bruce, Bob, or whatever his name was very into you." Sue said, raising her brows suggestively. Eva did not want to let her best friend on the big secret, which not only was he not into her, but he also only wanted to get into her. Literally.

"Yes, well I have standards, so I think I will be a little more patient."

"Oh yes of course." Sue began drily.

"Your knight on his big stallion, get over it and stop reading romance novels, it will never happen!" That's Sue never wanting to look past the surface and only the shell.

Wanting to change the subject Eva said, "So what are you searching?"

They both sat down on the mini sectional. Eva was looking around, taking in the beautifully decorated apartment. Thanks to Sue's inheritance they managed to decorate the apartment like a hot New York style loft. Everything is chic and modern from one brick wall in the living room with its surrounding walls in a soft orange. Stainless steel sculptures scattered throughout the living room kitchen and a huge window overlooking Manhattan.

"Well I know this is Mr. Rich IV, but I think he is almost too perfect. One thing I never did before was look them up on Facebook or anywhere else. I know it sounds creepy, but by the time I want to get serious, the Mrs. pop up and it is just me and my broken heart left in pieces." *Now she was using her pretty head.* Eva thought.

"I am glad you decided to do something before things started to heat up, let me know if I could be of assistance."

"So how has your days been in hell with Gretchen and company?" They have these conversations when she returns home, and it is always the same thing. Only the last couple of days, something did happen, sort of.

"You would not believe it, it's almost insane. I was on my way to finish up for the day when Mrs. Carter came in with a proposal." Eva said, wiggling her eyebrows.

"Oh an indecent proposal!"

"Ha!" Eva said excitedly.

"Nothing too indecent actually, she just wants me to babysit one of the people at her house party they are having in a couple weeks. And she's giving me three freaking grand!"

"That's good Eva! As long as they aren't sacrificing you and selling your body parts, I'd go for it." Both ladies laughed.

Out of breath, Eva mentions, "I was also in the library finishing up, and Mr. Carter comes in yelling about one thing or another. I could not believe how handsome he was. I know I see him in passing sometimes but this was different. And besides that, he is rude as all get out. So, after he not so gently reminded me, I am the cleaning lady, I left out quick. I almost wanted to quit. He is now a certified dip stick."

"Look honey, I would have made sure dismissing me was the last thought on his mind, learn to use your beauty. You could have men eating the forbidden apple right out of your hand." She paused.

"Anyway, I am going to dinner with Kevin later so do not wait up." Sue winked as she sashayed off to ready herself for class. Eva felt a stab of jealousy when she saw how happy Sue was. She had everything. She was not too tall and not too short. Her long hair was beautifully colored with different blondes and browns naturally. Eva was certain that Braxton would love to be with her even if for one night. Eva studied English at St. Francis College and minored in Environmental Studies. A nerd, as some would say. She knew this, but it was two things she was

passionate about. Before heading out, Eva changed into her long

black sleeved shirt with jeans, the suggested 'please burn me'.

Eva put her hair into an all too familiar bun to complete her Plain

Jane look. With little time to spare, she opened the boxed

package that was left by Mrs. Carter. Inside was a beautiful teal

silk dress, slippers, and an additional set of clothing. A note was

nestled inside a clutch silver bag.

Ms. Evangeline Brun: I am excited that you have agreed

to participate in this very important endeavor. Lady Scarlet is a

very important contributor to our cause and it goes without

saying that you are fit for this effort. She enjoys literature as

much as you do and has a penchant for ethnic figures. I trust you

will represent us in a good light and remember the stipend that is

being offered. If you have any questions reach out to Jeffrey

~M.C

As Eva was wondering more about this mysterious gathering, her

phone began to ring with a call from her good friend Jason.

"Hey Jason."

"Hey Eva! You would not believe the news I have."

He sounded so excited she kept her voice steady despite her mood for the day. "Well, you know I could try to guess but we would be on the phone until God knows when."

"I was invited to take part in planning this year's Victorian Masquerade Charity ball!"

Oh I am jealous for the second time today. Penny corrected: 'It *would be the third time if you included the lady who was entertaining you, no who?'* This ball was one of the most elite parties of the year. With well over two-hundred people in attendance. *He is definitely favored by God.* "Wow Jason, I am super excited for you, this will really put your name in the books for future planning." There was a pause.

"Eva you want to come? I have another complimentary ticket."

"Jason where is the question? Of course I want to come this is awesome." She never thought she would be a part of something like that. She always read historical books about balls and just imagined herself there. Today's balls could not hold a candle to the romantic style centuries ago. Her alter ego was telling her *this is our dream and maybe you can slip into a dark corridor with Braxton.* "Eva, you still with me?"

"Yes, I was trying to figure out if I was still dreaming." "OK, the date is set for June 6·, we will talk more about it later on I have to get to class. See ya when you get to school." Eva jumped up and thanked God and did a little dance. This was going to be the best night of her life. As she was dancing, she started thinking, this was less than two months away. She'd have to purchase a dress, her rags would never be able to fit in this crowd. *Where is my fairy godmother when I need her?* Sue walked in dancing behind her.

"So why are we dancing? Oh look at that dress."

"I'll tell you all about it. Come on, before we are late for class, today is finals."

■■■

In class, Professor Goodwin was going over Dubliners by James Joyce. The short story that was used for the final was Araby. "OK graduates, I am making this final easy and straightforward. Number one I am ready to go on break and two I am certain you all are ready to partake in the goodness of adulthood. So, let's keep it simple." He paced back and forth. Eva was happy for this gem, and with everything that happened these last two days she was having a hard time concentrating on anything but the Carter's Residence. While the professor was still talking, she winked at Sue and Jason and told them good luck.

"Any questions?" The professor stared pointedly at Eva. She was caught again daydreaming. She raised her hand to justify her blank stare. "Yes Eva."

"Just to clarify we are going to critically analyze Araby's narrative voice such as the ending lines where he says, "Gazing up into the darkness, I saw myself as a creature driven and derided by vanity, and my eyes burned with anguish and anger'."

"If I were you Eva I would stop talking, you are writing everyone's' paper if you keep it up, but in short yes that is exactly what I am looking for and a very good example." Eva looked down at her Bluebook ready to finish this chapter and start a new one.

Chapter Four:

Braxton

Braxton threw the tabloid down, hating the paparazzi and so-called journalists. He wondered if they ever read The Elements of Journalism. He probably should have purchased this book with Bill and Tom he thought. He assumed it would give credence to whomever comes up with these false tales. Half of what they say is completely false and the other half only half truths. In the mist of his fuming, his mind reverted back to the beauty that was definitely a hellion. He was caught off guard by how much an instant attraction to her. One thing a man of his position has always done is not mix business with pleasure. It has been a while since he has been with a woman and chalked up his desire for the hellion as just that. Amongst other cardinal rules of a bachelors was: Never sleep with a virgin, never take on a romantic date or any date, and never spend the night in a private home. Living by those standards has given him a piece of mind for the last sixteen years. As if in a queue, his phone rang from an unsaved number.

"Hey Braxton, it's me…Elizabeth, I was wondering if we can get together soon?" He glanced at the number again, hearing a familiar soft feminine voice. *Ah, the Italian.* He mused.

Braxton just thinking that it has been a while since he has enjoyed a woman's company said to her, "I will send a driver to pick you up later around 10:30 tonight."

"Oh…" she stopped and started again.

"I was hoping we could grab dinner, but if you are too busy then I will see you tonight." He heard the sadness in her voice. He made strict rules when it came to his lovers and at this point sticking to the bachelor's Cardinal Rules has always served him well. Instead of encouraging feelings that were non-existent to him, he says he will see her later. Thinking he would get a moment of peace, his father came in the library with piercing silver eyes like his own. His look sent solar flares right through him.

"Braxton Carter, what were you thinking and who was that woman you were with?" Not stopping for Braxton to interject," he continued.

"You are bringing too much shame on this family's name." His father was beaten red pacing angrily to and from, stopping only to pour himself a glass of whisky. Braxton did a once over of himself in the mirror behind his father. Ironic. He was thinking of a thirty-one-year grown man being lectured on proper behavior by Mr. Whore himself.

"I am sorry to disappoint you father, however, that is complete bullshit in paper. I am working on buying Miss. Anderson's company before it goes belly up." He was nearly screaming at his father. "Be that as it may Braxton, having yourself in those situations should be a lesson. Everything should be done in a proper setting with etiquette. If you keep this up there will be a trail of women that have been allegedly sexually harassed by you. Better you take care now to not ruin everything we have built." He paused as if in heavy thinking.

"You need more responsibilities and that I hope will keep you in order. We will announce the plans at our annual donors' event and after the Victorian Ball, your stepmother and I are going to retire to our estate in Scotland. You will be the sole owner and CEO of Carter Enterprises, as of this moment grow up and be a damn man." With that, his father chugged the whisky and stormed out of the library, leaving Braxton with his jaw to the floor. This was not what he wanted, he had his life going in the right direction for him flaws and all.

He left his family's mansion to go to his penthouse in Manhattan's financial district. He knew what he needed: A ride on his Icon Sheene. He loved his bike. Silver and Platinum. He commanded the road whenever he took it out. Braxton rode his motorcycle hard for hours before finally stopping at Elizabeth's apartment in Brooklyn. He had a couple hours before his driver was supposed to pick her up. *What the hell?* He thought. Now is as good a time as any.

Chapter Five:

Evangeline

Evangeline woke up panting for air as another dream about sex invaded her senses. She walked to the window gazing out at the sky as the lightning illuminated the beautiful Manhattan skyscrapers, followed by a loud crackle. She pressed her forehead against the chill of her window, thinking about the man who intimidates and engulfs her senses since the embarrassing moment he found her in the library. Even though she avoided him for the last week, she was unsure why her body and mind were responding to him after their brief encounter. If one could call it that. Eva tried to will herself to summon up the memories of her dream. Instantaneously Penny leans against the window saying, *it is because you would love nothing more than a man of his caliber to notice you and make you completely his.* Her mind was racing with so much what ifs as she decided the best remedy to ease the tension in her body was to write in her diary and create a poem while listening to Beethoven's Moonlight Sonata.

Dear Diary,   *April 14, 2012 5AM*

I have been having so many mixed emotions running rampant in my mind, I never thought I would be the type of woman to fantasize about a man who is not remotely interested in a person like me, how could he be my dear friend diary, I am all messed up inside. Scarred from a past that I cannot remember. A heritage that will haunt me until my very last breath, it amazes me that I allowed society to make me feel so abnormal. It must be why I am so infatuated in a time where everything was so screwy, I wish I could go back and say to the world we are all the same. Anyway, it has been a rough journey, and I am happy that I will start my career this year. Graduation is coming up and I know I should be ecstatic but I will not have anyone there to clap for me or to hug me and say they are proud. It hurts my dear friend diary it hurts. Until next time your everlasting complainer.

~Eva

Eva closed her diary and really had a mental breakdown. The ball is about a month and half away and with the dinner party funds Eva will have according to her calculations will be a total of 12,000 dollars. This was all thanks to Susan who charges pennies for rent. She thought the whole ensemble would cost 1,000 dollars minimum for something decent or she could wear the teal dress that she would be wearing to the dinner party. Her decision was made. Eva hated to spare the expense when she was saving for a used car to purchase and a down payment on her own apartment. Right as she was about to give up and commence with her breakdown, she recalled she could potentially ask her mentor to borrow a dress that was used for plays with time given she could have it tailored for a fraction of the cost. *Yes, that solves the problem.* She mused. Thinking to herself, one problem solved and another rooting up from within, how would she keep away from the man who has been haunting her dreams for the last couple of weeks?

The next day sleep evaded Eva again, so she busied herself to clean the apartment. Susan wanted to hire a cleaning service but Eva did not feel right about having her best friend spending too much money, when to her money was just too important to waste doing something one could do on their own.

After what seems like hours into the early morning, Susan finally wakes up and comes into the kitchen to sit on the barstool.

"Hey, you want some coffee?" Eva asked her. She noticed her friend was a little puffy eyed, so unlike Susan, but Eva figured it had something to do with Mr. Rich IV. Rather than intrude, she continued to make breakfast.

"Kevin said that he loves me." She blurted out followed by a burst of fresh tears. Eva went to her to comfort her thinking of the right words to say.

"Well, what is wrong with a declaration of love? Not too many people are handing those out these days." Eva's alter ego pursed her lips. "He said that right after he decided that we should move on because of our age difference. *Ouch.* Eva says in her head. "Eva, I think that I am really in love with him."

"Just give it some time Sue, he is probably scared shitless by your independent nature, you know many rich guys do not seem to like that." She smiled.

"I will take that coffee. You know, you really are the greatest friend I have ever had." A lonely tear escapes running to Eva's sharp jawline.

"I will always be here for you." Sue swiped at her cheeks in full composure mode just now.

"So how are the preparations for the Victorian ball? You have everything you need? I have been so busy with my speech for graduation, I did not think to ask you."

"Well, I am waiting to hear back from my mentor, hopefully she will allow me to borrow a dress otherwise I may have to cancel with Jason or go into my savings for my car. However, I only asked her yesterday evening so there is still time."

"That is nonsense, we have one hour until Florence is in her shop, we will stop there and no arguing."

She gave Eva her pointed stare that generally meant her way or nothing. "Thanks Sue, I will pay you back."

She said, putting the final touches on their breakfast. While they were eating, Sue brought up the dinner party.

"So, Eva, you have the whole ensemble from Melony, its four days away, have they given any more insight on this Lady Scarlet?" With a mouthful of spinach omelet

Eva replied, "Well not exactly, I just know that I am to go there on the 18. at night so that I can greet her early the next day, they are supposedly coming in on the 18. as well but just retiring and no entertainment."

"Does Braxton know his mom asked you to be there?"

"I'm not sure although I cannot say for certain why she would, it seems as though I'll be attached to this woman's hip."

"Interesting" Sue added as they finished their breakfast and prepared to leave.

They were both on their last stretch of college life as undergraduates, Eva deciding to take a permanent vacation from the cleaner service after the dinner party, she applied for an internship at the university to become a professor's aid as a means for graduate credits. They walked down Manhattan's shopping district to the Madam Florence boutique. The boutique was beautifully decorated on the inside. Small and furnished in a French Pavilion theme. Furniture in creams and ivory. A mass of fabrics lined along each side of the walls varying from silk, cashmere, and satins. Florence hurriedly flocked to Susan's side smelling money.

"Madam Smith, a pleasure to see you again and so soon. What can I help you with?" All lights and beams when Sue come in, Nevertheless, Eva could only surmise at how expensive the outcome of this trip will be.

"My best friend in the whole world will be attending a Victorian ball at the Elite Palace and we need her dazzling from top to bottom and underneath." She said, wiggling her eyebrows.

"Madam Smith, I will be honored to make a dress and unmentionables!" She shrieked.

"Well, I guess we better get started!" Sue said laughingly, Eva rolled her eyes and giggled. Florence whistled to a few of her associates and after a while together they came up with a silk silver dress with a high waistline along with several layers underneath to give it the Victorian era look, but chic as well. A low-cut bodice that was of course a tad bit bold for Eva's taste. Eva sat down finally while Florence went over the final designs with everything going over her head. Sue sat bubbly, sipping champagne.

"Sue, you know you are such a good friend, really I am glad that I met you, and you and Kevin will get through this rough patch." She paused.

"That is what this is you know." Sue looked at her a little uneasy.

"Eva, I hope that one day you do get your fairytale ending." She smiled sadly.

After hours upon hours of mind-changing designs, Florence decided to incorporate small glass diamonds along the length of the dress. They settled for a black masquerade mask that would have some silver glass diamonds surrounding the eyes. Immediately Eva thought the dress resembled the color of Braxton's eyes and wanted to change the whole concept but backed out when she saw how happy Sue was to be doing this for her. Florence said this will be her priority and will have everything made up in a few weeks. Eva gave Sue a quick hug and together they left for Sue's hair stylist Roderick.

"Sue how about I pay for this trip, I will not be taking no for an answer." Along the way, Eva discreetly gained Kevin's number to tell him a thing or two.

As the two left the salon, Eva was glowing. Roderick really did a number on her. He gave her feathered curls down her back and threaded her eyebrows. He made sure to tell her to see him and only him. On the taxi ride home, they talked about graduation and final exams. Upon coming home, there were two dozen roses by the front door, Sue looked at Eva.

"Don't look at me Sue, I'll likely receive my first bouquet at my funeral." Eva smiled coyly, Kevin must have gotten and thought about her message. Susan picked them up and read the card.

I am scared but more afraid of letting you go -Kevin

She smiled at Eva handing her the card.

"Eva they are from Kevin." Eva read the card as she was opening the front door to the foyer."

"What did I tell you Sue, call him now!" Eva went directly into her room muffling sobs she choked down. She was really happy for Sue. She deserved to be happy especially with her parents always comforting her with money rather than love. She was glad she texted Kevin and more so glad her best friend was happy again. After a few moments it took to compose herself, Eva went into the kitchen and fixed them Chicken

Alfredo, shortly after returning to her room to fall asleep from exhaustion.

Thunder roared its ugly head causing my breath to come in a heap, I am shaking uncontrollably in the corner of a small confound space. I heard and smelled blood mixed with death as the thunder was continuously calling. I feel someone taking my hand and thrusting a locket into it, while sitting me gently inside a crate. I look up and it is my mama, my mother! I open my eyes wider as she closes the lid and I wail and I wait and then nothing, just the sound of thunder and a light right beside my ear.

"Eva are you OK? Sue turned on the light and came into her room. A look of complete terror on her face.

"Oh Eva, you had another nightmare did you forget to take your medication?" She climbed into her friend's bed and wrapped her arms around Eva after giving her the pill. It had been quite a while since she had these dreams. Six months to be exact. It was always the same thing. Her therapist, who she saw once a month because of the expense, prescribed her Ambien.

Which is sleep inducing medication. It also helps put Eva in a

hypnotic trance while sleeping, decreasing the strength of REM.

Chapter Six:

Sue

It had been a day and a half since the nightmare that
shook Sue from her sleep to find her friend whaling shaken with
cold sweat. She had only witnessed this incident a handful of
times since Eva and she became best friends and moved in
together. Those night terrors that claimed her friend's inner
peace leave Eva somewhat drained. However, today was the day
of her dinner party and Sue would not let her miss it. She made a
cup of coffee for Eva and knocked softly on her bedroom door.
"Hey sleepy head, it's almost two in the afternoon and you have
a dinner party today." She smiled down at her holding out a cup
of medium roast Donut House coffee. *Mmm It smelled delightful.*
Eva thought as she inhaled the aroma.

"Thanks Sue, er…sorry about waking you up the other
night, I guess with all the excitement yesterday I forgot to take
my pill." Sue was the only other person who was aware of Eva's

her nightmares, other than the therapist and the screwy orphanage that she spent fifteen years in.

"It is OK Eva, I just wish you could talk about it with me. I have known you for four years and you have not said a word besides when you mumble in your sleep." Sue cocked her head to the side as if she was recalling one of her episodes. "I actually remember one time you sounded like you were speaking French." Sue was fishing for information, but with the dark circles beneath her friend's swollen eyes she needed to try to get her to open up. Without commenting on Sue's reference of French, Eva hopped out of bed walking to the kitchen, hoping that Sue would just drop the subject. Sue shrugged her shoulders and followed behind Eva.

"Kevin and I decided to give it another shot, he wants me to come for drinks tonight at his club…" She paused. "Why don't you come with?" She took a long sip of her coffee.

To her surprise Eva agreed with one condition, "I'm shopping in your closet." Sue shrugged.

"You know where everything is, help yourself, I am going to have my own little dinner party tonight. With the father and his girlfriend, who I might add is our age!"

"I would hate to say Sue, but Kevin is knocking on the door of fifty. Can't beat em' join em' huh." They laughed as they both gathered their things to head out for the day.

Chapter Seven:

Evangeline

Eva came home the following day exhausted from the dinner party. It wasn't as bad as she thought. Lady Scarlet was an interesting woman. Although, her infatuation with ethnic cultures was a tad bit uncomfortable for her taste. Eva went into Sue's room that swallowed the other one so far as the extravagance. She had a chocolate tufted headboard made from a beautiful oak in the shade of mahogany. A huge armoire, dresser and a vanity are set to die for. Eva walked into her massive closet, everything perfectly organized according to fabrics and color. The bottom layer consisted of shoes of all different types.

Eva wanted to wear something classy and appealing at the same time. *Was there even a way to do that?* She decided to just pick out some ivory linen pants and a pair of five-and-a-half-inch Fendi chocolate heels with a one-inch platform. This was the only thing that was remotely decent to her that would match her dark brown silk-capped sleeve button up. It was the only item in her wardrobe that she never wore and was the most elegant. Outside of the teal dress courtesy of Mrs. Carter.

****

Susan returned home from her afternoon run and immediately began to shower and get dressed. As the time neared nine p.m., she began to get dressed wanting to back out of going. The last thing she wanted was to be a third wheel, but this would be her first opportunity to meet Kevin and she made a promise to Sue. Susan came into the room thirty minutes later looking like her usual gorgeous self. She had on a canary yellow mini chiffon dress accented at the neck with a metallic choker. To her the dress was much too short and thin.

"Eva, we have to go, why are you not dressed?" She rolled eyes. "Unwind your panty's will you, I just have to put on my clothes, and we can leave. Ten minutes top." Susan gave her an appalling look. "Eva! Ten minutes is not even enough time to pick the right shade of lipstick! We have thirty minutes minimum." She walked out mumbling that she needed a glass of wine. Eva shook her head. *Jeez.*

She loved her friend, but she is always so over the top. She quickly dressed haphazardly, buttoning her shirt all the way to the top. Eva thought the pants were too tight. She went over to glance at herself in the mirror. *Yes, too tight.* Her alter ego made an appearance, shaking her head disapprovingly. *Your buttons are not aligned and gosh get a life it is just a butt!* Before she could adjust the buttons, Sue walked in taking. She unbuttoned four of the buttons, leaving her honey-kissed breast peeping through the top.

She gave herself a chocolate and white diamond necklace with matching earrings and bracelet. "You are not a nun get over yourself, you will never meet someone dressed like that! Now sit down so I can do your make-up." Eva did not want to respond to those comments as far as she was concerned, she was not a nun nor a strumpet. As she completed her mini transformation, Eva looked at her reflection thinking that it was not so bad. Sue already knew not to put too much make-up on her, so she put on a little bronzer, mascara, eyeliner, and a soft shade of nude matte lipstick from Zahara Red Cosmetics. Eva marveled at her entire five foot six inches thanks to the mega platforms and felt stunning.

■■■

They arrived at Whites, an upscale club owned by Sue's boyfriend. Eva walked in feeling slightly overdressed compared to the other women in attendance. Directly in the center of the club was a bar crowded with people getting inebriated. A glass elevator was on both sides of the club that led to the second and third levels. The club was quite crowded despite this being a Tuesday. *This is what rich people do, gather on a Tuesday and get tipsy.*

Whites was a massive club, ultra-modern with black and white scattered sofas throughout the first floor. What caught Eva's attention was the astonishing pearl half-winged piano sitting on the stage. Strangely, it seemed out of place. Susan was ushering Eva towards Kevin for an introduction. "Kevin this is my roommate and best friend Eva, Eva this my Kevin." She stopped looking embarrassed by the Freudian slip, revealing her inner possessive feelings for him. They shook hands as Susan was shining all smiles and a rose blush upon her cheeks.

"Nice to officially meet you Kevin."

"Likewise, Eva." "You can call me Evangeline."

Eva excused herself for not wanting to feel like a single loose thread on an otherwise perfectly designed blouse. She went to the bar and ordered cranberry juice. It was lame, she knew, but this was as good as it was going to get. As she scanned the host of people, she saw the very man who disturbs her dreams from afar. Braxton. He looked devastatingly handsome in his black suit jacket, crispy white button up and jeans. *Oh my!* Penny said as she slid across the winged piano. *He looks so damn sexy, go talk to him. Remember your little interaction at the dinner party!* Eva immediately dismissed that notion, for it was better to gaze at him from a distance. A red head plopped down next to Eva, obstructing her perfect view and even pretended to look at the drink menu, while she was casting side-glances at her eye candy.

If Eva thought Sue's dress was tiny, this wanton fools was only an inch from her butt being visible to all those around her. She rolled her eyes and started taking in the scenery. She saw Sue and Kevin nestled up in a booth heads pressed closely together like lovers sharing an intimate secret. A few other people sat on the sofas chatting away. As she swiveled her barstool to where Mr. Drop Dead Gorgeous was, her eyes locked with his as he made his way in her direction. Eva being self-conscious was thinking that he was coming to flirt with the red head. Her mood soured.

He came and told the bar tender to pour another round for the red head and herself. She could not help the aroma he gave off. A mixture of pure man, soap, and *oh Armani!* She turned to the bartender, her legs slightly grazing his, the small touch sending quivers down her spine. She was about to spark up a conversation with the bartender and thank him for buying her another juice, when he spoke. "Hello ladies." His voice was holding the right amount of sensuality accompanied by the perfect baritone pitch.

Just the sound with those two words warmed her inside and out. Redhead smiled wickedly at him and crossed her legs so he could get a full look at her scrawny thighs. She reached out her hand not waiting for Eva to speak. "Hi to you, I'm Eliza." *Oh, she has a Russian accent, how the heck was her hair red? She wins*, Eva thought. "Nice to meet you Eliza." He takes her hand and shakes it and turns to her with a half-smile. His silver eyes held hers for a second He was too perfect. Perfect hair. Perfect teeth. Perfect skin. That's just perfect. *Ever heard of love at first sight? Well, second, third? Who's counting anyway?* He took Eva's hand caressing her knuckles. "And you are…?

He finally moved his lips again to speak. Red head girl quickly says at the same time Eva does, "going to be sick." "She is not with me." Eva glared at her for a moment, deciding to go outside to get some air. *Ugh, did he think he was getting a threesome? Arrogant prick.*

Outside Eva wanted to kick herself. "Going to be sick really!" She said aloud, pacing back and forth in front of the club's entrance. What was she thinking? She being lost for words that was going down in history. She wove her fingers through her silky hair, her spirals were still intact despite the humidity. Granted it was thick, but she liked her tiny spirals that sprang when it was wet. She took her phone out of her purse to text Sue about the embarrassing moment along with her ZRC lip balm. Before she could finish her text message, someone came suddenly upon her pointing a gun at her back and directing her to the side of the club.

She quickly looked around, but the streets were deserted, except for this low life and her. She looked towards where she thought was heaven and prayed that he did not rape her. She attempted to talk calmly to him, letting him know he could just take her purse and go. "Sir you do not have to do this, just take my purse and go, I promise I won't look back or scream." Eva tried to put confidence in her voice. "Shut up bitch! Just move." She began to panic hoping that someone would come outside for a fresh breath of air.

He started speaking, "Où est la clé?" He was speaking French and she did not understand what he said. He grabbed her hair, spun her around, and slapped her across her face, hence the term bitch slapped. "I do not understand what you are saying." She was near tears more frightened than she had been in her whole life. "Do not lie little peasant girl, where is the key?" He was about to slap her again. She screamed.

Chapter Eight:

Braxton

He never would have thought a woman would make an excuse to walk away from him. Usually, all the women flocked to him. *Maybe she had too much to drink.* He saw her across the room standing out like the reddest rose amongst a field of tumbleweed. She looked so exotic he could not put his finger on her nationality. Was she Brazilian or Egyptian? Not American. He had never seen a more tantalizing and beautiful woman in all his life. He wanted to get closer and admire her closely.

Maybe she would go to a hotel suite with him. Braxton dashed those thoughts out of his mind. A woman dressed like that was not interested in one-night stands. *There is always a first time for everything.* He was getting a whole speech together in his head, when the lovely red head came over to sit next to her.

Before he knew it, he was giving them his million-dollar smile. The red head fought for his attention. The beautiful one slid from the bar stool a foot shorter than himself. After his miserable attempt at introductions, she walked out of the club saying she was going to be sick. He looked dumbfounded at the bar tender and picked up her drink to smell its contents.

"Cranberry Juice?" He looked at the bar tender who was equally as perplexed.

"Mr. Carter she only had one cranberry juice." Forgetting about Eliza, he headed outside. Although he was a silent partner in this club, he did not appreciate if someone slipped her a drug in her drink. He left through the front entrance seeing that she was not out front.

Braxton scanned the usually crowded street, which was now completely deserted. All was quiet for a moment until he heard a woman scream. Adrenaline pumped through his veins as he rushed in the direction of the voice he heard. He saw a hooded man about to strike her against her face.

Just as he was about to hit her with what looked to be a gun, Braxton did not hesitate. He would not allow another woman to be a victim while he still held breath in his lungs. He grabbed the man's arm and they both exchanged a few punches, until finally he was able to get the advantage and knocked the man unconscious on the ground. Braxton pulled out his phone and called the police notifying them of the incident and their location. He picked the gun up using a handkerchief placed in his suit pocket.

Chapter Nine:

Evangeline

She could not believe her eyes, one moment she was making piece that she was about to get raped and beat because that guy assumed, she was someone who had something of his. This is why she never went out to places like this. It was like a candy store for all the perverts and men who thrived on a woman's vulnerability. Braxton came out of know where to save her life. Even though it was mid-spring, shivering she felt like she was standing at the tip of an iceberg. Eva took the hand that Braxton was offering her as she moved from the arms of the cold brick wall. She wanted to collapse against his chest and cry. She wiped her face with the back of her hands as he pulled her away, keeping her at arm's length.

"You must be cold, take my jacket."

Oh my gosh why is he doing this? He wrapped his jacket around her, running his hands up and down her arms. She was in a daze as she looked at his silver eyes, which were darkening as each moment passed. She smelled him on her the familiar aroma of Armani and soap.

He was speaking to her, but she could not speak. He ushered her into the club and spoke to two guards telling them to wait outside with the fallen man. He escorted her into an office on the first floor that she did not notice before. She blinked rapidly as her adrenaline started to shift. Her cheeks burning from the sudden change in temperature or the close proximity of this Greek god standing close to her. He put a glass to her mouth and she obediently drank the dark liquid, as it burned down her throat. She choked. "Excuse me Mr. Carter, I do not drink." He lifted his eyebrow. "Frequently."

She took the glass from his hands surrendering to his silent command. "This will help you calm down a little, who did you come here with?"

"Sue, she is my best friend, her boyfriend's name is Kevin, I believe he is the owner." He walked out the room and she looked at her reflection from the mirror anchored across the room. She could see a slight bruise on her cheekbone, she was trying to run her fingers through her hair just as Sue came in.

"Honey, oh my God are you all right?" As Sue was walking over, she could tell she had one too many alcoholic beverages tonight.

"I'm fine you do not have to worry just give me the keys I am just going to go home."

"Of course." Eva already expected her to not come home tonight. She took the keys from Sue's hands while hers was still a little shaky.

Braxton came in at that moment. She looked into his compelling eyes, feeling herself losing a battle that hadn't even started.

"Mr. Carter did those men happen to bring in my purse and phone?" "Unfortunately, when they went outside the perp was already gone, they managed to bring in these." He handed over her phone and her Zahara Red Vinyl Lip Lacquer.

"And please it's Braxton." With their fingers lightly touching, she yanked her fingers back like his skin hot oil in a frying pan. "Oh no!" She said panicked. She put her pills in her purse not wanting to forget them at the scheduled time. Her nightmare was no doubt going to come rearing its ugly head.

"It is OK honey, I will be there with you tonight." She did not want Sue there tonight, when she knew that her dreams were an inconvenience and something she wanted to keep as private as possible. They hugged again.

"It is OK Sue, you have fun I have spare ones at home." She whispered in her ear. Breaking their embrace, Eva said, "I am fine. Really, go back to Mr. Rich IV, I was not hurt."

She immediately regretted the words as they came out remembering they were not alone. Braxton raised his eyebrows to her again. She flushed a magnificent cherry. Sue gave her a quick hug and thanked Braxton on her way out swaying a little.

Eva began to walk out of the club when a police officer and his partner stopped her.

"Excuse me Miss we need a statement from you." *Oh shit!* Penny yelled. Not only would he ask to see her license, which she did not bring, he would get her name and find out she was in a club, underage, on top of all that she would blow above 0.0 thanks to the disgusting drink Braxton coerced her into drinking. *This does not bode well for anyone here, especially Kevin.* She quickly thought of something.

"Officer, I really do not feel up to this tonight, can I just come in tomorrow? I have a blasted headache, if you need a description the owner is here tonight you should talk to him about getting a tape. I did not see that guy's face my purse was taken along with my identification."

Surprisingly, he gave her his card and told her to follow up or use the Telephone Crime Reporting system. She thanked him and his partner again, walking away to Sue's car. While she was fumbling with the keys in her purse, she felt someone standing close by her. Right away her body had become tense, and she started shaking. *Not again.* She turned slowly. It was Braxton.

"I did not mean to startle you, are you friends with Kevin's girlfriend? He and I are family." *What am I supposed to say, crap how am I always lost for words every time I am near him?* She nodded her head, not answering any question in particular. "Anyway, I feel it is my duty to drive you home."

Oh. Penny starts to belly dance around the Cadillac.

"Mr. Carter…It is…not a problem, I have not had much to drink at all tonight." Her voice lacked the conviction of her statement. "I insist, you are still a little shaken by what happened." With that he grabbed the keys and took her hand and led her to the passenger side door, leaving her unable to object.

The drive was more intense than the thug who tried to rape her. He pulled into her apartment's parking lot, for a moment, she wondered how he knew where she lived, then remembered he must have spoken to Sue or Kevin before driving her home.

He gave her the keys and she walked numbly to the door. She still had his jacket on and knew that it was really chilly out tonight.

"If…you want you can wait inside for someone to pick you up."

"Thank you." Braxton smiled at her and her insides went all warm and on cue she started blushing from head to toe. *This has to stop.* She turned, allowing him to pass in front of her into the foyer. She led them into the living room taking off his jacket, handing it to him, and already missing the smell of him on her.

"No, I should thank you Mr.…Carter." She stuttered again.

"Had you not come out when you did...?" She closed her eyes unwilling to speak further about the incident that could have changed her life. That did change her life. She just hadn't realized it yet.

Chapter Ten:

Braxton

He had no idea what compelled him to take her home when she was clearly not interested in him. But whenever he looked at her, she automatically blushed making her look more angelic than before. *This was going to be fun.* He had already told his driver to come in one hour. There was plenty of time to do what he had to do and leave. Kevin might hate him for it, but this was one woman he was not willing to leave behind. She cascaded past him into the kitchen, her scent seducing his senses during the whole car ride and still.

She smelled like vanilla, roses, and a touch of something smooth. She thanked him for coming to her rescue as he walked to the kitchen to grab her hand. Taking one of her small hands in his he said, "It was a pleasure Miss…"

"Evangeline Brun." She said while looking at him with her big brown eyes. *She was more beautiful and exotic than he realized.* He wondered right away how many men she looked at like that with her eyes and kissed with her full lips. Braxton brought her hand to his mouth to brush a kiss across her knuckles. He knew she would flame that brilliant cherry across her cheeks. He sat down on the barstool. "Miss Brun, I am just glad that I was there, and you did not get fully injured."

"Would you like some tea or coffee Mr. Carter?" *Tea or coffee eh.* Either she was completely innocent or good at seducing men. He preferred the latter, a true coquette. The former would not be too bad either. He did overhear her calling Kevin Mr. Rich something, maybe this was her and her friends' game. He smiled at her again.

"Coffee. Black."

Chapter Eleven:

Evangeline

All her current issues were put in the back of her mind as she retrieved two coffee mugs and K-Cups. She moved to prepare the coffee, making sure that everything was in order. With her treacherous thoughts running rampant again had her growing hot, thinking about his mouth on her hands and wanting them to be all on her at once. She was falling deeper and deeper for a man she knew she could never have. Someone outside her social class, a teenage love she should've left in high school. She should tell him right away she worked for his family cleaning their home and that she spoke to him multiple times before only he made no notice then. She didn't. She wanted this moment to last and there will never be a moment like this again. She thanked God that she did come across that fleabag tonight, otherwise he would have been with the red head for sure.

"So, Evangeline I assume you know a little about me seeing how you used my last name, so tell me something about you...school?" Penny wakes up sitting as if in a front row seat.

"I was studying Victorian literature and environmental science. I did work for your family once upon a time." She paused.

"I do not claim to know anything about you Mr. Carter, but of course I know some things, in the sense of what is said about you in the tabloids." She said the last words in almost a whisper.

To her surprise he tilted his head back and laughed. She noticed he had dimples. *Where did they come from?* All she needed was more to add to his already perfect form. She stood planting the coffee cups on the counter and slowly made her way to him like she was being summoned by Hades himself to enter the underworld. The lights were dim, and the setting was all wrong but oh so right. She was ready to give herself to him to hell while waiting. She may never have another opportunity like this. *What the hell?* He stopped laughing and pulled her roughly into his arms. She never thought she would get this close to this man. At closer inspection she could see in his eyes where there were spots of gray mixed in with the silver. His breath tingling her senses from the smell of whisky. She put her hand flat against his cheek, wanting to do that since the very first moment she saw him. He stood up and swallowed her with his height.

Before she could back out, he pressed his lips against hers, roughly at first his stubble burning the smoothness of her skin. When she gasped, he slowed the kisses down, probing her lips with his tongue, a silent request to enter with his. She opened her lips as his tongue explored the inside of her mouth. Matching his rhythm, she made an involuntary moan. He broke the kiss.

"You are so beautiful Angel." He nuzzled at her neck as he sat down on the stool again.

She felt his erection against her stomach. She knew that if he led her anywhere, she would follow. He gazed down at her while unbuttoning her blouse. She put her chin down ashamed of her body and her behavior. He tilted her face up to look at him.

"Do you know how insanely attractive you are? I want to fuck you right now, do you understand?" She locked eyes with him again and they were getting darker by the minute. He kissed

her. She would be satisfied with just that. He caressed her breasts

through her blouse as she moaned again, louder than last time.

He growled into her mouth at her response to his touch.

Eva knew this was the moment she would gamble everything

and accept what he was offering her. A quick fuck. His phone

rang. Caught in the moment she thought he would not answer.

Whoever it was, was being persistent, and it brought her back to

reality. She stepped back so that he could answer his phone.

"Carter." He snapped. She heard a woman's voice on the

other end. She was completely thawed from being frozen in time.

He walked into the living room speaking in a hushed tone.

"What do you mean you are at the club…damn it…put

Nathan on the phone…" She could not hear what he was saying

but he looked angry. He snapped the phone closed before dialing

another number. He is back in business mode.

"Where are you…? I am coming out." She looked at him

pleading with her eyes for him to stay and to continue what he

started.

"I have to go Angel, there is an issue at the club." Eva didn't understand what that had to do with him as Kevin was the owner and he was the only family. She started buttoning up her shirt with all the dignity she had left. Fingers shaking, barely feeling the fabric.

"Of course." She muttered, her heart shattering. He was going to go be with one of his many women. She gave herself a mental slap. She could have been added to the number just moments ago. He must have seen the look of disappointment in her eyes.

"Can we pick it up from here?" He said as he trailed his finger across her cheek. There was hope or there was just her wanting to make something out of nothing.

She grabbed a sticky note from the computer desk in the corner and wrote her number down. He took the paper and left her standing in the middle of the room with one last kiss that ended too soon. Blindly walking back to her room, she collapsed on her bed like a sack of potatoes. *Did I really just give him my number knowing he left to be with another woman?* She pondered that question until she drifted off to sleep.

Chapter Twelve:

Braxton

What the hell was he thinking? He knew for sure he was going to grab Melinda and head home to take a cold shower. *Evangeline…no Angel, it suits her better.* She knocked him off his feet. He knew he should steer clear of her, she could only bring a man trouble. Not just beautiful but an intellectual weakness. A weakness he had never experienced before.

Joe was intent on driving while he was lost in deep thought. Thankfully Nathan had Melinda secluded in his office.

When they arrived at the club he was fuming, partly because of the exotic beauty he left standing in her living room, her lips swollen from his kisses. The other half was standing right in front of him.

"Linnie what the hell are you doing here?" Braxton snapped at her. She swayed slightly.

"God are you drunk!"

"Braxton, I don't know about God, but I had a few glasses of wine." She made her way towards the door. "I am going to go and dance the night away, leave me alone."

"I cannot deal with you right now, Nathan, take her to the estate."

"Sir." He muttered as he took Linnie away. What was he going to do? His father put him in a terrible situation, there was no way she would behave on this side of the globe.

■ ■

A few weeks later

Braxton sat up in bed for the first time and felt unsatisfied by the woman next to him. Elizabeth slept soundly after a not too gentle fuck. She was just what he thought he needed to keep his mind from going to Angel. Instead of her green eyes under him, he saw Angel's big brown eyes begging him to take her to the next level. Braxton was rougher than he needed to be, his mind kept drifting back to the way her kisses called him like a siren in the lake driving him wild, losing himself in her memory. He had not been able to get in contact with her due to this month's business needs overshadowing personal pleasures. *Maybe I need to fuck*

Angel to get her off my mind and rid this longing to have her screaming in pleasure. Yes, that needs to happen and soon.

Chapter Thirteen:

Evangeline

Her dress finally arrived a day before the ball, after a quick examination of the dress, she thought it would look beautiful on her. Over the last three weeks, she was a little taken aback that Braxton had not made the slightest attempt to contact her. She was still ashamed of herself for being so willing to sleep with a man who she barely knew. Granted she saw him almost every day for the last two years and they had multiple conversations, although he did not know it was her. Eva grabbed her phone so she could touch base with Jason.

"Hey Eva what's going on?"

"Oh nothing, I was just checking in on you. I know you have to be at the ball a little earlier to set up, I was making sure you don't need help."

"Yea, I am on my way over there now it is going to be great. What are you wearing so that I can meet up with you?"

∎∎

"Now, now, Jason what is the point of a masquerade if you are going to know what I am wearing?" She teased him. It was easy to talk to him. She enjoyed their playful banter.

"Eva you are going to be bored out of your mind, you do not know anyone there…but suit yourself I will find you." Her phone beeped with an incoming text from an unfamiliar number.

"Yea, yea I will find you later Jason." She hung up the phone and went to her inbox.

■ ■

Hello Evangeline, this is Braxton Carter and I was wondering if we could get together tonight.

B. Carter

Her insides were all in tangles as she remembered kissing, touching, and the weeks of no contact. She went cold. Immediately recognizing what this was. An invite to have sex. Her coldness turned to anger. However, she knew she could not solely place blame on him for making the assumption she was into this type of thing. Before she could respond he texted again.

I was hoping we could pick up where we left off…

B. Carter

The famous dot dot you fill in the blank move.

Mr. Carter, I humbly regret that I cannot meet with you tonight, I am engaged this evening.

Eva B.

Who the hell does he think he is? I am not some whore bag. The night he came to their condo was a major mistake and a poor lapse in judgment that she did not plan on making ever again.

I like rain checks Angel!

B. Carter

Oh my.

Either he is horny as hell or he just wants to get her to sleep with him to add to his growing number. *I don't think so.* She put aside her phone not wanting to further recall that humiliating moment. Eva refused to text back.

Chapter Fourteen:

Braxton

She had plans. He mused over that all day. As it neared time for the ball to leave, he had the pleasure of escorting his sister Linnie. Although he tried to put Eva out of his mind, he kept thinking about who she was otherwise engaged with last night. A low growl surged through his throat. *Where were all the possessive thoughts coming from?*

He knew for certain that he needed to be intimate with her to get her out of his mind. His focus should be the ball tonight. The event will raise money for urban areas that lack funding in New York. The funds would provide extracurricular activities for free, summer camps, and eventually education advancement programs. He checked his phone every five minutes not believing that she turned away from him again, only this time for sex. That was a first.

Chapter Fifteen:

Evangeline

Sue had just finished applying Eva's make-up which she allowed her to take further this time. Sue brought out the big guns. Transfer proof cake mix foundation by Beautie Bakerie, Zahara Red Cosmetics kiss proof red liquid matte, and a Gucci limited edition highlighter. Sue put spiral curls on her hair and pints most of it up. Eva looked like she could have really lived amongst the aristocrats in the mid-1800s, except for her never-ending tan. Eva purchased glass diamonds, which were more expensive than they should have been.

"Eva, I must say you look fabulous, when Braxton sees you tonight, he will be utterly smitten with you if I must say so myself." Sue gave her a quick twirl and her silver dress hugged her body like it was nobody's business.

"Sue I am going for two reasons. One it will be an amazing experience to add to my portfolio and two Jason needed a sidekick. Not to mention Mr. Carter and I hardly know each other. And besides, I am not interested in sex calls." Sue raised her eyebrow.

"So, he invited you for hot steamy sex and you said no, are you crazy!" Eva corrected her.

"No, he did not. I am saying that had he, I would have definitely said NO!" *It was halfway truthful.* The doorbell rang she assumed it was the driver that Sue paid handsomely for so she would not drive her Cadillac, which as she put it, would clash horribly with her silver ensemble. She put on her mask and looked at her complete transformation. She could not recognize herself.

■■

Eva arrived at the ball at the Elite Palace, everything on the exterior and interior was covered with lavender roses and pops of ivory throughout. The entrance, manned by two men in costumed footman livery, bow ties and white gloves. The ballroom was flooded with all different types of people. The wardrobe of everyone there was magnificent. The ambiance of the ball was such that she felt like she was at a 'real ball' during the reign of Queen Victoria herself. Instead of crystal chandeliers beaming with electrical light, there were hundreds of candles that set the scene of a love nest. She giggled to herself. *How many maidens were ravished back in time in the dark corridors without a chaperone?*

Feeling bold tonight, like Emma from Jane Austen's novel, Eva walked over to a server and took a flute of champagne. Taking a sip, *it was marvelous*. She made her way around the ballroom, being stopped by random women who complimented her on her appearance. She finished one flute of champagne, grabbing another feeling less and less shy and more coquettish. One of the hosts alerted everyone on the speaker to go into the grand ballroom for the night's first waltz. Eva learned to waltz from one of her classes. It was a requirement as part of the Victorian education 101. The orchestra was softly playing Ludovico Einaudi's primavera, *it was such a great piece*. She stopped to compliment a man on his suit, he smiled down at her and wrote his name on her dance card. She spotted Jason taking pictures of guests wearing big white wigs. *Now that was something.* Eva perhaps, would not have worn it even if she lived in that time era.

Eva walked over and poked Jason to his side. As he finished taking the picture, he turned towards her muttering an "I'm sorry Miss." Then turned around. She poked him again this time with her hands on her hips. "Eva is that you?"

"Of course, it is." *Was I that unrecognizable?* "You look stunning my lady." He took her hand in a mock bow and she curtsied. She took his hands in hers and said, "I cannot thank you enough for inviting me." Jason took her dance card.

"Just save me a dance, I am surprised your card is not filled up yet." She grabbed another champagne flute from a passing server.

"That is probably because I have not sat down long enough for someone to approach me."

"Well, I have another round of photos to take before I can take a break, we will catch up then." Jason started to walk off then turned back saying,

"Eva easy on the champagne you are a lightweight remember."

"Yea yea." Eva turns. She sees him.

Penny, with perfectly timed bad advice, awakens as she turns around and sees Braxton writing his name on a tall woman's dance card. He leaned down and kissed her on the cheek. Eva lost in thought as usual, thinking this was the woman who interrupted what could have been the best night of her life. *It still can be.* Penny rants at her. Eva knew she should not be here at this ball staring intently like a brazen she-devil at Braxton. What was the alternative? He was the most beautiful man she had ever seen. He was tall, broad shouldered, with unique silver eyes, and dark chestnut hair.

Tonight, he wore his hair slicked back just long enough to be tied back at his neck. Braxton looked nothing short of regal. *Prince Harry.* He completed his look with a tailored long tail black suit with a matching silver waistband matching the allure of his prince charming vibes.

Eva felt herself warm underneath her mask as she was mentally stripping his clothes off of his body. Suddenly he looked up, locked eyes with her, and started in Eva's direction.

She quickly glanced down, ashamed of where her thoughts were going.

"Excuse me Miss…" she was struck dumbly.

"E..va.." She replied, staggering her words a little bit like a drunkard on the street. The light of recognition lit his silver eyes. "Miss Eva, I have never seen you at one of these functions before. Granted, it is always a masked affair, I am happy to make your acquaintance."

"Mr. Carter it is over two hundred people here I am sure you do not see every one of them."

Darn it! She thought.

Now he knows she was staring at him and knew who he was BY LAST NAME.

Anymore lame and I'll be needing a crutch. Eva wanted to melt, his gaze seemed to penetrate into her. Why does she always have to be awkward and rhetorical? A ridiculous combination. He tipped his head back and laughed, showing off a perfect set of pearly white teeth. She was in trouble.

Chapter Sixteen:

Braxton

Braxton was amazed at how she looked tonight. Hair pint up with a few curls escaping, and a silver diamond accented dress hugged her sweet curves in all the right places. His blood boiled momentarily as he saw her from across the room being hugged by another masked man. Before he could stalk over and claim she was his, his sister came over to coerce him into dancing with her. Following their small conversation, he said, "Would you do me the honor of the first waltz of the night Angel?"

Before giving her a chance to answer, he ushered her unto the dance floor as the sounds of Johann Strauss II played softly.

"You really are a great dancer Mr. Carter."
She looked at him with beautiful brown eyes. He could smell the sweetness of her vanilla rose perfume and a tinge of Moet on her breath.

"Evangeline, please if you insist on looking at me like that, then you have to call me Braxton." He swirled with her to the melody, his eyes never leaving hers as they both consumed the dance floor as if a fire was burning within their circumference. He thought they molded well together, with clothes on. He looked at her with blazing silver eyes. "Angel you look absolutely beautiful tonight." He stopped and dipped his head into her hair. "And you smell wonderful. I wonder if you taste as good."

Chapter Seventeen:

Evangeline

Evangeline looked up at Braxton blushing profusely. *This really must stop.* What was he trying to do? Penny edged to her side saying, *he is trying to get in your panties, so let him.* "Mr. Carter, I do not know you and I am really sorry if I gave you the wrong impression the last time we met. But I am not emotionally or physically available right now."

There she said it, might as well get this over with. She glanced down avoiding his eyes so that she wouldn't regret the words said that she knew to be right. Eva made a move to leave his arms and leave this place before she fell deeper in love with a man who could never love someone like her. As she tried to turn away, he gripped her closer, pressing her body into his. He whispered in her ear.

"Miss. Brun, it just so happens that I am emotionally unavailable as well. You can decide on the physical part you can decide that." He winked at her. It was not until it was too late that she noticed she was being led from the ballroom floor and swept into the lobby, to a room that was lit only by the moonlight. As soon as Braxton opened the door, he pressed her against the door, pinning her there with the length of him. He tilted her chin up to look into her eyes, unspoken words promising moments of bliss that would come.

He kissed her softly, teasing her lips with his tongue, until she parted them, and he invaded her mouth with his. Their tongues were swimming together in a slow duet. She moaned and arched her body towards him, her breast rubbing against him. He made a growl. As he took off her mask, he began planting kisses down her throat. Eva reached up and took his mask off, curling her fingers in his hair and pulling him down to give him what she hoped was a passionate kiss. She was rewarded by a thump of his erection. She moaned involuntarily. *The champagne must be giving her courage*, Eva mused. There was no way that she would be brave enough to do this in a sober state of mind.

Chapter Eighteen:

Braxton

Before Braxton exploded in his pants, he reluctantly pulled away, missing the absence of her in his arms and seeing the burning desire set deep in her brown eyes.

"Angel I want to take you right here, right now, but there is someone I bought that I have to take home. Please tell me you will come to me tonight. I cannot think straight until I have you." His eyes pleaded.

Chapter Nineteen:

Evangeline

Eva could not believe what she was hearing when she saw him come in with a woman. *But he danced with her.* She pondered. Maybe they have one of those freaky open relationships. Her stomach turned into knots and before she could stop her hand from moving she slapped him across the face.

"I am not one of your little whores Mr. Braxton Carter, you have humiliated me for the last time. I suggest you take your feeble mind elsewhere and seduce some other woman. Perhaps the one you brought and leave me the hell alone!" Eva snapped.

Braxton stood rooted to the ground dumbfounded and confused. No one had ever dared call him feeble minded let alone slap him, *women!* He thought. She must have thought he was here on a date, which never stopped a woman before. He smiled again, his Angel jealous... He stopped smiling, *since when was she his Angel.* He stood over her, not speaking, waiting for her to calm down. She didn't. Instead, she turned around and left him standing alone.

Eva stormed back into the ballroom glancing this way and that hoping to catch a glimpse of his date so she could tell her… *tell her what,* she thought. T*hat she was in love with her boyfriend… That she spent the last half hour making out with him.* Shaking her head, she said *no… tell her what a cheating bastard he is.* She should already have known what type of guy he was, everybody knew, but when he looked at her as if she was made of gold it made her feel warm and tingly, feelings that she should not expect to have.

"Angel you are blushing." Braxton said as he lifted a finger to her cheek discreetly. *How the hell did he get over here?* Eva must have been daydreaming again.

"Get your filthy hands off me." She hissed quietly. She saw the tall woman coming in their direction not wanting to stand and watch him touch the woman the way he was touching her. She walked out to the garden grabbing two flutes of champagne.

Chapter Twenty:

Braxton

Braxton recalled her telling him that she did not indulge in alcohol. Pondering at her actions tonight, he did not hear his sister talking to him.

"Brax, what is going on with you? You have been distracted for the last couple weeks." He led his sister off the dance floor and grabbed them both champagnes. He took a swallow knowing he would need something stronger tonight. "I was preoccupied with an issue at work, nothing I cannot handle." He surrendered her to a group of women that she happened to know. First telling her that he would be going to his penthouse instead of the family estate, so she could leave with Nathan.

He walked around looking for Angel, he did not want someone to take advantage of her tonight. She seemed to want to be drunk senseless and this was not the party to do that at. Right before he went out to the garden, he spotted her with the man from earlier. Laughing and smiling before being swept into a dance. His blood was boiling as he was sizing up his competition. *Evangeline was no good for him. Hell, he was not good for her.*

But he could not resist being drawn to her. He was going to go over there, take her from that man's arms, and take her to a hotel suite. Yes, that is what he would do. As they circled the floor coming closer to him he saw her staring directly into his eyes and saw hurt. He did not understand women and their emotions, which is why he had his rules. He and emotions just don't go together. *Therefore, what was her problem? Surely, she knows what this is.* Her friend Sue was not a subtle type of girl. As the saying goes, you are who you hang with. Braxton did not get why she was acting so virginal. Maybe that was her play. Playing hard to get was overplayed and a game he did not want to be part of. He stood in front of them, cutting off their circle.

"May I cut in?" He said more to her than the short guy she was dancing with. She let her hands fall from the man's shoulder and turned towards him, taking the other guy in hand.

"I'm sorry, we were just leaving." She said a little too harshly for his taste. Before he could respond, she was dragging the guy behind her like a puppy. Braxton found himself wishing he had snatched her back in the room to tell her she was misconstrued about his situation, anything other than to see the anger and hurt that her eyes blasted at him. But this was all for the better, he surmised. *Yes, better for her.*

Chapter Twenty-One:

Evangeline

"Hey slow down Eva." Jason was panting closely behind her. Eva gave the valet her tickets soon after the driver came to pick them up.

"What is going on?" Looking Jason in the eyes, Eva noticed for the first time how handsome he was. Blue eyes and a killer tan. A little on the short side but still uncomplicated and emotionally available.

"Jason let's go somewhere. This place is super borrring." Eva slurred her words.

"You are so tipsy, it's kind of hot." *See.* Eva thought he thought I was cute.

"We could go to this after party it's at a club downtown."

"That's cool Jason I want to get completely drunk tonight! I cannot wait." At that moment, the driver came around and Jason directed him to a club in Brooklyn. Eva turned up the music listening to something that she was sure would give her a

headache had she not been drinking.

"JASON... you areee a cool dude mannn."

Jason smiled. "Sue is going to kill me."

■ ■

They arrived at a small club much too crowded for its

capacity. The music was loud, Eva could feel each beat within

her body. She gave the bartender her credit card and told him to

run a tab.

"Jason tonight is my treat, you got me into the ball it's

the least I could do." Almost feeling normal again, Eva was

having a second guess at coming here but she needed to get away

from Sue and her happiness, and Braxton with his, I just want to

fuck you personality.

"I won't stop you" Jason winked.

"You ready for a real drink Eva?" She nodded her head.

He ordered four shots of whisky for them. Eva immediately felt

the effects, but she was happy. Wondering over to the dance

floor, she danced with a tall guy, *very sexy* she put in her head.

Just what she needed to get her mind off him. Penny sprang

fourth with her pumps on.

The way you let loose Eva your heart is racing, you're

stomping on a five-hundred-dollar dress. Oh, yesss baby! After

the fourth shot of whisky Eva found Jason talking to a group of

women and told him she was going to the restroom. Although

she was intoxicated, she would not make the same mistake by

going outside for air. *Especially without Braxton here to protect*

me. She shook her head at the inward thought. The bathroom

was by far the most disgusting place she ever saw. Paper towels

littered the damp floor, and soap was poured on the sinks.

Ughh. Animals. She wandered towards the back of the

club and found a small utility closet. Feeling like a brazen animal

herself, she picked up her phone to call Braxton and give him a

piece of her mind.

"Hello." Too late to hang up she heard his deep voice

sounding like I just had mind-blowing sex. That heated her up

more.

"Braxton…youuuu are sexy too sexyyy for yourrr own

good." *Wait.* That is not what she wanted to say.

"Evangeline is that you?" Are you drunk?" He had his papa bear voice on now. She could hear him talking to someone in the background, *his whore*!

"No, I'm not drunk!" she snapped talking louder than necessary.

"I'm sick of you, sick of thinking about you." She slurred her words together. "You think your God's gift to women, but you are a rake, and I love you sooo much." She stopped. Burped.

"Sorry, I meant I hate you." She was crying now.

"I'm going to find a guy tonight to take my mind off of you for good." With that, she hung up. Finding a bottle of water on the shelf, she drank and splashed water on her face. Her phone buzzed again.

"HELLO."

"Evangeline where are you?" Braxton hissed into the phone.

"Oh Braxton go to hell where you belong."

"Evangeline where the fuck are you?" Eva quickly hung up and marched back into the crowded club to find her sexy tall guy. Rather than get the drink he offered, she ordered a bottle of water and bar snacks. They sat at the bar talking about plans after they left. Eva, as she sobered a little, began to regret taunting Braxton and leading this man on.

Chapter Twenty-Two:

Braxton

Braxton was furious as he was driving fast to get to her before it was too late. *What was too late?* He contacted Kevin and he inquired with Sue about her location. Thankfully, Jason, the guy she was with at the ball had the decency to let her friend know where they were going. Thinking of all the trouble she could get herself into he sped past red lights wanting to be the real-life Dr. Strange. Who was he kidding, the thought of her leaving with a stranger angered him. It should not matter, she was nothing to him. Nothing.

Parking his car at the front of the club, which appeared to be a no parking zone, he raced into the club. Hair mangled from tossing and turning for the last few hours. Braxton looked around the club and saw the guy she was with earlier. He went to him asking about her. Drunk out of his mind, he had no clue. He turned around ready to shut this place down and he spied her being caressed on her ass by a greasy head man. He stormed over and lifted her out of his embrace. The guy pushed Braxton slightly back, but his body didn't budge. Braxton looked as if he was ready to tackle him as Eva tripped and almost fell.

"Hey man what's your problem?" The unknown man said.

"You are touching my wife and if you touch me again, I will beat you senseless." Braxton rose up to towering the man with his six feet four inches. The guy threw his hands up.

"Hey dude no disrespect, I didn't know she was married."

Chapter Twenty-Three:

Evangeline

Eva could not believe her ears. His wife. Her wit coming back, she said, "Yea I didn't know either." She rolled her eyes, it might have been too dramatic an action. Her brain being fuzzed by alcohol, she stood up as tall as she could, taking her heels in hand. By then the sexy tall guy had left, she was standing square up with Braxton.

"I'm not your wife, you sleazebag!"

"Thank God!" He spat back.

Chapter Twenty-Four:

Braxton

Taking her arm, a little too tightly he walked almost dragging her behind him. Planting her feet on the ground was a sure mistake, he dipped and picked her up across his shoulders with little effort. This was making her dizzy. "Braxton! Braxton!" she shrieked.

"I will walk OK!" Reluctantly, he put her down in front of the car and leaned his head down on the hood. Eva slid to the ground, head in her lap and began to shake and then vomit. Her hair was getting in her way. She felt a warm hand rub her back and pull the hair from her face. Gagging willing her stomach to empty the rest of the toxic drink from her soul. Finally, when nothing else seemed to come out she stood with the help from Braxton, while he took his handkerchief from his jacket and wiped her mouth. Their eyes locked, unresolved feelings stretching between them. Eva felt her insides grow warm and tingles in places she knew she should not have.

"Thank you, Braxton." She gave him a weak smile and fell forward, Braxton catching her in his arms.

Unbelievable. He was furious at her and the guy who brought her here. *How could he let her get so damn drunk?* He laid her in the car and tried to get her conscious to drink water, but she kept babbling.

****

What am I doing? Braxton brought her to his penthouse that was a stupid mistake. He felt he should have, knowing that she did not drink and if he was not going to have her then damn if that grease ball would. He was watching her sleep like an angelic hellion, the moonlight spilling across her body. Braxton was taking his new role seriously, using all his strength to be immune to the perfection laying across his bed in a soundless sleep. He slid into the bed with her putting a pillow between them drifting off into a tortured sleep. Or so he thought.

Chapter Twenty-Five:

Evangeline

It was a horrible smell, my noise burned with fumes

unknown to me. I slowly opened the crate clutching the locket my

mama gave me. Slowly I stood looking around the small, boxed

home. There she was lying open-eyed, staring at the ceiling,

bleeding so much, her hair matted to her face. I shook her,

calling her name, she would not move. Mama, I cried repeatedly.

A hand grabbed me from behind and I screamed.

"Angel… Angel wake up." Eva opened her eyes to an

unfamiliar setting. Shaking from the dream she just had. The

only thing familiar was the voice. She turned towards the voice

and saw Braxton shirtless, staring at her like the freak she

ascribed to herself. Eva glanced around the room and saw what

looked like a bathroom, leaping from the bed and slamming the

door behind her. She sank to the floor and cried.

What was she going to do? Eva looked down at herself

almost naked in the bed of the man she was completely

consumed with. She did not remember anything that happened.
Did they have sex? How did she get with him? The last thing she
remembered was dancing with a guy and being thrown over
Braxton's shoulders as he stormed through the door. *Oh My
Gosh!* She realized as memories flooded in for her, she called
him and had gotten ill outside the club. He tried to open the door.

"Angel are you OK?" He paused. "Come out, it's five in
the morning… you need to sleep." She knew for sure she was
not going back to sleep to remember…*what exactly*. She could
pretend not to remember the horrid scream she knew he heard.
She went to the sink and splashed some water on her face and
proceeded to drink a cup of water.

Opening the door, Braxton stood up from the bed in only
his pajama pants hugging his waistline. His sexy hip lines
showing. His chest was bare, with eight rectangular shapes lining
vertically down his abdomen side by side. His chest was
sprinkled with hair. He looked so beautiful. *Could you describe a
man that way? No, he looked like a God. Not as it relates to
religion, more like Greek mythology. Zeus.*

"Um...could I borrow a shirt from you?" Suddenly conscious of her body. He walked over to the dresser and pulled out a crisp white shirt.

He walked over to get her a t-shirt. Much to his chagrin, he wanted her to stay just the way she was. The body of a goddess. Aphrodite in the flesh. Full breasted and curvy in all the right places. *Her hips were a perfect handful just enough for a man, no, me.* Just enough for him to pick her up and put her against the wall. His friend stood to attention at his inward thoughts. He tossed the shirt to her and walked out of the room. He knew she would have a hangover. He went to the kitchen first for a bottle of water and then the medicine cabinet for Tylenol. He came back and gave her medicine and a bottle of water. She was wishing that he would just put a darn shirt on. She was tempted to walk over to his dresser and get him one too. Not able to stand the silence longer, she blurted the first thing that came to mind.

"Did we have sex?" Braxton's look was not amusing.

"No Evangeline we did not." *Okay, that was a relief.* Moving to sit under the blankets on the bed because the temperature seemed to drop at a constant pace.

"So why am I here? And where is here?"

"You are here because you called me. This is my home." *OK.* She remembered calling him not what the conversation was about. She wanted to pretend like she was sleepy, hoping he would take the hint and let her fall back to sleep. Her head was pounding. Inadvertently she put her fingers to her temples and massaged them.

"I'm sorry I called you, I didn't mean to mess up your date." He looked at her eyes darkening.

"Actually Miss. Brun it is I who should be apologizing, it seems like you were about to leave with your dark-haired friend last night." She cocked her head to the side, her memory slowly coming back in pieces from the few hours that lapsed. She remembered him telling a guy that she was his wife, and that horrible phone call. *Oh my gosh!*

"Do you remember?" He asked. There was no way she was going to admit to being that ridiculously childish. "Um… No, I cannot remember a thing." That seemed to satisfy him.

"It's probably because you are still a little fucked up, you want to talk about what just happened?" She shook her head slowly, memories of her dream coming back to her.

"OK, you should go back to sleep, I will have Joe take you home after you've rested." Instead of telling him she could not go to sleep, she sank down in the bed, turning away from him. Trying to keep a steady breathing pattern harder than she imagined. She felt him turn around to wrap his arms around her and she failed miserably with the breathing exercise, her heart was palpitating rapidly.

"You are not sleeping, are you?" He stated more as a fact than a question.

"No, I cannot." That would be an understatement. For the first time she felt secure and safe like her dreams could not haunt her in this man's arms. But she was afraid, afraid of dreaming.

"Whenever I have a bad night, a hot shower helps out. The other thing is better, but a shower is still good." He stood up going to the bathroom and turned on the shower. Eva followed.

"Thanks Braxton, I know it's early and you have a million things to do." She was glancing in his magnificent silver eyes. "I do not have a change of clothes, I think it is better if I leave now." Penny popped in the middle of the bed. *What an excuse.* He looked at her and walked from the room, returning a couple of minutes later with an all-white cashmere jogging set.

"Here you can wear this, I will go make coffee." *His girlfriend's clothes how nice.*

"I really do not want to wear that." He looked her up and down, mischievously.

"It's OK, it's my sisters I don't think she will mind." He turned and walked out. *His sister?* Eva did not realize he had a sister.

The shower felt so good. She took a bottle of shampoo from Seventh Generation. Eva knew she would probably regret washing her hair, but she could smell alcohol and cigarettes all over her body. She turned the shower off and wrapped herself in the softest towel she had ever felt. She was starting to get cold from the shower so she right away went to the clothes he brought. Looking at the price tag she almost fainted. *$650.00 for* *a jogging suit WTF.* Not wanting to put on the same underwear from last night, she went to his dresser and fumbled through his drawers until she found his basketball shorts. By the time she was done dressing, her hair was going into mini spirals, shrinking to become her familiar curly afro.

Chapter Twenty-Six:

Braxton

Braxton was surely going crazy, starting with entertaining Eva's phone call. He was thinking about her waking up screaming and sweating and wondered what would be troubling her so severely. Just then Eva walked into the kitchen and saw Braxton fumbling with the coffee machine. He looked like he never used it a day in his life. Fortunately, for her she and Sue had a similar machine. She reached over him, grabbed one of the two cups on the counter, and grabbed the V-cup, their hands slowly touching each other.

"Mr. Carter if I didn't know any better, I would assume you never used this kitchen robot." He was staring at her again. *Did he not know how that made her feel?*

"Eva you would be right with your assumption." Without further elaboration, he went to get cream from his refrigerator while she made them two steaming cups of coffee. Taking a sip, Eva exhaled.

"So that is one thing the world would be fascinated to know." He raised an eyebrow, cocking his head to the side.

"Mr. Braxton Carter the genius of green technology, cannot make a cup of coffee."

She giggled. "You should do that more often."

"What…tease you?" He chuckled. "No laugh."

"Well, it just so happens Mr. Carter, I do laugh quite often, just not around you."

Looking perplexed he said, "Why is that Eva?" Penny hopped on the counter sipping a latte.

Oh, because you make her feel intimidated, desperate, and safe. Shaking her head and not wanting to say any of those things, she just complimented him on his taste in décor noting the eco-friendly touches. This was something important to him," she gathered. She never saw a person so happy in explaining in minute detail everything in the house. He offered to take her on a mini tour.

Apparently, most of the products he had were prototypes that his company is working on to help make the world a little greener.

"So that is what you do Mr. Carter, I never perceived you as the 'let's improve our planet" type of guy." She paused.

"I thought you conservatives did not believe in global warming." He looked a little agitated at that last comment but did not say anything. He continued to show her his living room first which was off the kitchen. He had solar powered blinds. When the sun and temperature are at its peak, it retains the heat and slowly releases it into the home as needed to keep the thermostat at a constant temperature. A plus, he said, was that it allows the natural rays of light to come in and when it's dark outside they turn into a semi-transparent black.

The glass on the floor was made of recycled glass. He had a black winged grand piano off the side of the fireplace. It was similar to the one she saw in Whites. Twelve feet of art stood along his walls, making the room look more like a gallery. They made their way to the library which was equally as beautiful. It was the same as the one she used to clean and dust daily.

They ended up in a theater room with an 82-inch projection screen complete with leather reclining theater seats. She took this opportunity to sit down.

"Your home is immaculate Mr. Carter! I do not understand why you let everyone perceive you as a bad guy with no brain when you are clearly doing things that is actively benefiting the world." He sat down next to her.

"Eva please call me Braxton, and I don't care what people perceive me as, I'm not doing that so people can look at me differently. The people where all these things I am doing matter, they know who I am and what I do." He paused.

"Those are the people that matter." Eva wanted to say she didn't know those things until now. *Does that mean she doesn't matter?* Penny emerged with popcorn in hand. *He is a winner. Sexy, Tall, Rich, and he has a brain. Give him a kiss would you!*

"I never thought about it like that Mr....er Braxton... You really are a great guy it's a shame you would rather be known as Mr. Playboy than Mr. Sexy Genus."

Oh, did she really just say that? She blushed right away not daring to look at him.

Fumbling with her cup, his voice dropped low as he spoke. He lifted her eyes to meet him.

"So, you don't really think I'm a devil?" He knew he should not tease her like this, but he could not help himself. When she came into the kitchen, her hair was like a silk bouquet of spirals all around her face. At that moment, she looked like an Angel that fell from heaven. He still did not understand what made her have that terrible nightmare, he wanted nothing more than to kiss away that look of dread on her face. The same look his mother had. He needed to be inside her right now to ease the madness he felt for her.

"Um… I do not think you are a devil. I think…." Penny to the rescue. *Tell him what you think, stop behaving like an idiot. Tell him…*

"You're smart, beyond sexy, a great kisser, and." She stopped, *oh shit.* Did she just say that aloud?

The next thing Braxton knew his mouth was consuming hers. He pried the cup from her fingers and she right away brought them to curl in his hair. He pulled her to straddle his lap, not breaking their kiss. He started kissing her slowly wanting to take his time for the first time in his life. He kissed her throat, moving to her ear and gripping a handful of her soft curls in his hands.

"Angel, you are so beautiful." His voice was filled with passion. He slipped the shirt from her body, both almost completely bare but her in a lacy bra. Braxton moved his mouth, kissing the top of her breast slowly and teasingly. Eva moaned before he even started to work. He unclipped her bra expertly, letting loose her perfectly shaped breast. He took one in his hand while caressing the other with his tongue. He felt her legs tighten around him on the edge of an orgasm.

"Not yet Angel." Braxton whispered in her thick mane.

Why is he stopping? she thought. Her body was feeling too moist, and she needed a counter pressure at her core. She started to rub her lower body against him as he was kissing her breast and nipping at her. Then he stopped and the familiar ache began to crawl towards her honey pot.

"Why are you stopping?" For a moment she thought he finally came back to reality and realized she just was not his usual type. She saw the tabloids and the woman he supposedly had rendezvoused with.

"Angel do not over think, I don't want you to come yet…I did not realize you were so sensitive." He smiled at her dimples on display.

"Oh, I'm not usually, it must have been the shower." His smile faded. She knew he misinterpreted what she was saying. He picked her up, carried her to his bedroom, and laid her on his bed. This is definitely the day and oh was she happy.

"You are making me do crazy things Angel." Eva glanced up at Braxton, his eyes were now a smoky gray filled with complete passion.

"Oh really!" She pulled him down, cradling his head between her small hands.

"Evangeline, I'm not good for you and I don't want you to have expectations that I know I cannot provide." Eva was aware that he was giving her ample time to change her mind before anything got complicated, so she gave it a thought.

What did he mean? This was not a declaration of love.

But how often does a woman get to make love to someone that they are in love with for the first time. Before she would over analyze things, she pulled closer to him again starting their kisses slowly.

Their tongues swirled into each other's slowly a tornadic spin of heat and cold, she was greedy, wanting to speed up the pace, but Braxton, in what little self-control he had left, wanted to take his time. He dropped kisses along her jaw and her throat, finally finding his destination. He dipped his head to suck on one breast at a time hearing her moan beneath him. Braxton kissed and licked all the way down to her pants line, slowly removing the obstruction from his goal. She was squirming her chest rising faster and faster.

Eva was out of breath with no exercise needed. Now she was completely naked. The look in his eyes was not one of regret but of admiration. He kissed the inside of her thighs one after the other and slipped his finger into her folds. She gasped at the sudden pressure and surge of pleasure.

"Angel you are so tight." She moved her hips towards his hand not wanting him to stop the buildup she was feeling. Then he removed his finger.

"Are you always this ready?" He murmured hoarsely. Braxton gave her a quick kiss on her lips before returning to her sweet essence to continue his torture. Before she could react, she felt his tongue moving in small circles around her clit. Eva was biting back a cry that was trying to escape. And he stopped.

"Angel don't cover your face, I want to see you when I make you cum, I want to hear the passion in your voice, I want you to scream my name."

Braxton did not feast like this with every woman he was with. In fact, it was a while, but he could not help the scent that arose from her. She tasted so good he could devour her. He went back down to kiss her inner lips and felt she was on the verge of an orgasm. That gave him a newfound energy, he started licking and suckling until she started to move her hips towards his mouth, he inserted two of his fingers one after the other and she crumpled singing his name. Eva was extremely tight, if she had not said she was not usually this sensitive earlier he would have thought she was a virgin. She was gripping his hair and he was turned on. Still wanting to take things slow, he moved on top of her. He kissed her deeply, letting her taste herself on his tongue.

"Braxton...that was amazing." Her voice was husky from screaming and moaning.

"Angel I don't want to use a condom, are you safe?" Eva could not put two thoughts together in her head. Let alone comprehend what he was talking about. He must be talking about if she had an HIV test done. Which she did not because this was the first time all of this was happening. She nodded her head. She did not want to tell him that she was a virgin, not because she was scared, he would storm off, but because this was her moment and her choice. *Convention be damned.* She felt him readjusting his hips to position himself at her base. He slowly eased a little bit of himself inside himself as he felt a lot of pressure. Then he went deep in one thrust.

Fuck! Was all he could think of after he completely penetrated inside her, moving once...twice and came. *She was a virgin!* He knew something was all wrong from the constant blushing and her overly sensitive senses. He saw panic and pain envelope her face. He eased out and rolled to her side. The room

was filled with silence as he contemplated strangling her.

Looking down of himself wishing he were mistaken. The signs

were clear. Light pink blood was drying on him.

"Braxton what's wrong?" Still in shock, he rose from the

bed jerking on his pants.

She did not understand. From all her romance novels,

she knew that this was not the way it was supposed to end.

Bewildered, she pulled the sheet to cover herself.

"Hellooo!" She all but screamed. "Evangeline, I told

you I was no good for you." He snapped.

"What the hell does that have to do with this?" She was

completely at a loss and she did not understand why he was

reacting that way. Surely, he could not tell the pain she felt, for

men everything felt the same while they were in there. He

laughed drily.

"Really? Are you that dumb? You were a fucking

virgin!"

He paced back and forth from bed to window. She felt

like she was in the principal's office being lectured on the merits

of not cheating. "OK and your point would be what exactly!"
Now she was getting a temper of her own. *How dare he behave
as if she was asking him to marry her or trap him in anyway?*

"My point! My point!" She had never seen a person
angrier than he is now. She quickly stood naked and all. He
looked at her and immediately went hard again.

"I will not apologize for not telling you. It was not your
business and my virginity was mine. You are behaving like an
irrational child, scolding me for what exactly? I never asked you
to marry me or have any commitment to me. As far as I was
concerned, we did not need to speak or see each other ever
again!" She finished breathing heavily standing right in front of
him. Toe to Toe.

Braxton was torn between making love to her right on
the spot like he should have in the first place and running like
hell from the room. Not only was he mad that she never hinted as
to being a virgin, but he spilled himself in her in a matter of ten
seconds. His gaze locked with hers, he did not realize the door
suddenly was thrown open. Braxton stepped in front of her,
shielding her from view by the intruder. She peaked around his

body to see the woman from the previous night. She felt like a loose woman. Here was her rival and the man both of them wanted was just two seconds away from kicking her out of his home.

"Linnie, what the hell do you not know how to knock!" His sister had a habit of doing the unexpected.

"Sorry brother, I heard arguing and was checking up on you!" Linnie spat back at him, covering her face.

"I was not aware of you entertaining someone here." His silver eyes throwing daggers at his baby sister.

"Just leave Linnie, and do not come in my room again without knocking."

Pausing, he added, "And don't come to my house without notice, especially this early." His sister walked out not before slamming the door and making a picture fall from its place on the wall. Turning to Eva, he said.

"I have to go deal with my sister, you stay here we are not done yet." He pulled on a t-shirt and left the room.

His sister! Oh my.

She had not realized she, her invisible competition was his sister. And certainly not a full-sized adult. Granted he gave her the clothes and said they were his sisters, but this could have easily fit a junior high girl. Eva also remembered hearing something when she was working at their estate, but she assumed that she was in a boarding school somewhere and far younger than the beauty that barged in. All this time she was jealous of his sister. She was not going to stay in his home for one more minute. She called Sue.

"Hey Sue, can you come pick me up? I'm in the financial district in Manhattan." Her voice was shaky and tears sprang fourth at once.

"Eva its eight o'clock in the morning. What the hell is going on?" Not able to speak from the constant flow of tears, Eva managed to get out that she would tell her later at home.

Eva planned to go down to the main entrance, there would be a line of cabs waiting. Quickly putting on the borrowed clothes and stuffing hers in a small bag, she fled through the front door not wanting to see Braxton or his sister.

"Is this serious Brax?" Linnie sat at the stool in the kitchen, interrogating her brother. "You never bring a woman here, so tell me who is she?"

"She is nobody important now, mind your own damn business." Braxton snapped at his sister. He really was not in the mood to discuss his love life with her. He also did not understand what this was either. He ached to go to Eva and stop her from leaving, *for what exactly.* He had no idea.

■■■

It had been two weeks exactly since Eva fled his penthouse. It was just as long since he had any sexual relations. He tried, of course, but not one of his three lovers held any interest in him. Every time he closed his eyes, he saw only the pain and panic from her face when he shoved himself in her. Had he known he would have taken his time.

No. He would not have even been tempted to have sex with her. The lingering question that hung in his head, *well why do I keep thinking of her?*

■■■

Chapter Twenty-Seven:

Evangeline

Eva put all her energy into finding an internship, so she could jump-start her career. Granted, it was not her ideal internship. She spent four years studying Victorian Literature, and after events tied to the ball, it held little interest to her. She now wanted to intern at a company that specializes in green technology. Penny came saddened eyes and loss of weight. *Eva, you are doing this because it is something Braxton loved, just let him go!* Eva knew her consciousness to be true, somehow, she just wanted to hold on to things that never could be. It had been a little over a month, she should leave every trace of him behind, somehow, she felt a connection. The memories they had with one another she had to hold on to. Sue had to shake Eva's shoulders to get her attention.

"Eva did you hear me?"

"No, I'm sorry this job has me a little tired."

"I said, what have you eaten today? You are getting very thin and have terrible dark circles under your eyes. It's only so much that Zahara Red Cosmetics can do." Sue attempted a playful yet serious tone at the same time. These were the two things Eva was having trouble with. Sleep eluded her even with her medication and food held no appeal, especially after coming down with the flu. With all those issues Eva lost ten pounds in a month and a half.

Seeing that Sue was not getting through to her, Kevin interjected, "Tonight is the charity dinner for Green Works Foundation, you should come with us, before you try to talk your way out of it, think of the networking opportunities and it will be good on your resume." Kevin almost finished pleading. 'They had been good to her, Eva conceded and left out the room in her zombie-like mode. She sat in her room overhearing a hushed conversation between Sue and Kevin.

"Sue he is doing just as bad. I have never seen him work so hard in the last month. Sometimes he spends the night in his office." Sue snapped, "He deserves it how dare he led her on and not even call to see how she is doing!" "You know he asks us about her all the time." "That is not the point, and if you insist on taking his side why don't you start making love to him and not ME!"

Eva wanted to go to her friends and tell them not to argue and ruin their relationship over something that never was. She was starting to go across the hall and stopped short when she heard Sue moaning.

Well! At least they are going to have great make-up sex on her behalf. She did an about face and went to her closet to take out her graduation dress. Eva's long dark green silk dress was once again courtesy of Sue. After a quick shower, she put the dress on and left her hair in their naturally tiny spiral curls. She had started wearing her hair this way because Braxton told her she looked more beautiful than ever like this. She even put on a full face of makeup. She was tired of feeling sorry of being held responsible for a decision that was hers. What better way to slay than with Zahara Red Cosmetics glow palette Bloom into Beauty. After what seemed like hours, she went to the living room Sue and Kevin were already dressed. Both gapped at her.

"Wow Eva you look gorgeous." Kevin beamed.

"Yes, Eva you do, I'm so happy you decided to come out with us." Sue replied.

"You know Br…" Sue nudged Kevin in the ribs before he could finish.

"Thank you both." She gave both of them a hug.

"I know Braxton will be there tonight, only a fool would think otherwise and it is OK, it's also OK he may come with a date too." She took a deep breath.

"You both should stop worrying over me, I'm doing fine, and it is not as if we were committed to each other." They all stood in silence for a moment before getting into the limo. Kevin poured all three of them champagne.

"Let us have a toast to a wonderful carefree night." Eva took the glass although they both knew that she gave up drinking after the most humiliating day of her life. She raised her glass and drank a little bit of the champagne. The taste of it mixed with Kevin's overpowering cologne almost made her gag and she threw up. She closed her eyes and forced her stomach to behave.

"Eva are you OK honey?" Sue scooted close to her.

"Yes, I think that I still have a touch of the flu that's all." Sue and Kevin discreetly exchanged knowing glances at each other.

Chapter Twenty-Eight:

Evangeline

They arrived at the Manhattan nightclub called Avenue, it was magnificent on the inside, Eva could see right away some of the prototype green technologies that Braxton was excited about on stage. They went to their table as Kevin excused himself from speaking with a few investors. Eva saw that at the table were monogrammed name placements. Kevin Dole, Susan Smith, Evangeline Brun, Braxton Carter, Michelle Anderson, Melinda Carter, and William Chadwick. The name placements are all aligned together. *Couples in their love nests and she is alone.*

"Sue you did not tell me this was a couple's thing!"

"It's not, Kevin bought all the tickets and we all decided to sit together, and we did not even know if you were coming for sure." Before she could reply, Braxton and his entourage came over to the table.

Hanging on his arm was a tall and slender brunette. Her breast almost spilled from the top of her dress. Eva wanted to shrink to the smallest size possible, like Ant Man and run far away. She was not ready to face him yet it was too soon. As she was about to bolt away, Sue grabbed her arm lightly and whispered, "Don't run away he needs to see that you are OK, you have to see you are OK."

Standing tall, she squared her shoulders and put on a fake smile with Sue leading the conversation.

"Hi Braxton and company." Her rhetoric was aimed towards the brunette at his side, which according to the name placement was a Miss. Michelle Anderson. Taking Sue's hand, he put it towards his lips and kissed her knuckles.

"Hello Eva." His voice silky, caressing her body like the slightest touch from a newly bloomed rose. He looked into her eyes before bringing her hand to his lips and slowly kissed her fingers before planting a soft kiss on her palms. Eva felt herself flush again.

"Hi Mr. Carter, a pleasure to see you again after quite some time." Eva was reciting positive affirmation, saying she could do this over and over. That she could pull off tonight without being jealous of the beautiful older woman on his arm or the glances she was throwing at her.

"Everyone this is Michelle Anderson, a business associate." He stopped and looked at Eva wanting her to know that he did not just happen upon her. That their relationship was strictly professional and platonic. *My a*

"And this is my lovely sister Melinda." Everyone exchanged handshakes and Melinda said to Eva, "It's nice to see you again Eva."

OK. Eva needed some air to calm her racing pulse. Without saying an excuse, she turned and started towards the front of the building.

It was a nice and breezy evening in August for New York. Eva surrendered herself to the smell of late summer flowers that bloomed. She stood just thinking about her life, the plans she hoped to fulfill. Her phone buzzed. She saw it was a message from Braxton.

Angel, are you alright? I heard you had the flu… you look like you lost weight.

B. Carter

I am well, Braxton.

EVANGELINE

EVANGELINE is it now, will you save me a dance?

ANGEL

B. Carter

A dance huh…maybe, your date will be OK with that

EVANGELINE not Angel!

She realized how much she missed contact with him. She would do whatever she had to, to make it appear like she really was OK. With that, she walked back into the venue, head held high. Sue leaned in close to her.

"Are you sure you're OK?"

"Positive." She was as good as she could be with Braxton sitting next to her and the familiar smell of his cologne, made her warm and tingly down to her very core.

"Evangeline is it?" His Miss. Michelle Anderson spoke, laying a possessive hand on Braxton's arm and leaning forward. "Are you alright honey you are a little flushed?" Leave it to her to point out the obvious, which ultimately made Eva flush a deeper cherry.

"Actually, Michelle I have a natural disposition to overly sprayed perfume." She paused, looking directly at her.

"It's like if you can remember that long ago in high school when the girls piled a ton of perfume on or for recent memories, similar to a nursing home." Braxton choked on the champagne he was drinking. Eva turned her attention to Sue and struck up a conversation.

"Eva you are one crazy girl." They laughed.

"Well, you know what we say if we can't beat em join em." Eva stated slightly. It felt great for Eva to laugh again and for Sue to see her friend have a genuine smile. Things started to get to normalcy for them again. For now. Eva's phone buzzed in her purse again.

Well done Angel! But she is no threat to you…take it easy on her.

B. Carter

Braxton, I have yet to meet a woman who is a threat to me! Furthermore, there can only be a threat if we are an item (which we are not and will not be) You can tell her that I am no

threat to her is more like it!

Always Angel ;)

Braxton took a deep breath when reading her message.

She was doing it to him again, consuming all his thoughts. It felt

so good to see her again. He knew he should not have started the

playful batter between them, but the sparks between them were

still fueled and he was not ready to extinguish them yet.

"Hey why don't we all enter into the dance and clothes

auction?" His sister suggested to the women at the table. Sue was

excited, as was Michelle, by the idea.

"That is a great idea!" Sue agreed with Melinda. Eva, on

the other hand, decided not to participate.

"Sue, I'm going to sit that one out." The women struck

up another conversation and Braxton decided that it was the

men's queue to leave.

"Kevin why don't we go to the bar and have a real

drink." Kevin and William headed to the bar, his gaze never

leaving Eva. She was laughing and smiling at something his

sister said.

"Braxton you have it bad man." Kevin did not bother to hide what he was saying or whom he was saying it about. "Kevin we are just friends that's all." As he downed his shot of whisky, William piped in. "

She is one hot piece, what I will do to her." Braxton wanted to throttle the man at his side. Kevin spoke up.

"Looks like she is spoken for already Will." He tipped his head in the direction of their table. Braxton saw James Shepherd sitting down in his unclaimed seat flirting with Eva. James was a well-established French entrepreneur with a blotchy reputation.

"Kevin you should tell Sue to have Eva to stir clear from him." They both agreed that this was not the type of person that Eva should acquaint herself with.

Eva sat talking to this man something oddly familiar about him. He was leaning too close for comfort and kept putting his hands on her arms. She wanted to tell him to leave, but he said he was a friend of Braxton's.

"James you look very familiar I would swear we have met before." Eva felt uncomfortable in his presence and she wanted to figure out why. He looked old enough to be her father although he still held his handsome youth features.

"Evangeline, had I met you before I would certainly have remembered." The music started and people were slowly going to the dance floor.

"Miss. Brun if you would not mind sharing this dance with me." Eva was about to decline when she saw Braxton return and immediately Michelle started to pull him to the dance floor. Not wanting to be a wallflower, she accepted his hand as he led her to the dance floor.

As the orchestra played, they swirled around the floor, Eva's eyes glancing at the closeness of Braxton and Michelle.

"Evangeline you look quite preoccupied. I hope I'm not boring you." She looked into his blue eyes searching for the remembrance of meeting him before.

"No James, I'm just excited about the work that this charity function will bring." He gazed down at her, spinning her around and seeing just what was preoccupying her time and saw Braxton.

"You know Evangeline a guy like Braxton, is never good to get too involved with, why he has mistresses strung along the globe."

"James and here I thought you two were friends, warning me off of him." She tried to ease the nervousness out of her voice.

"I do appreciate your concern, but between me and you I do not fancy myself with him in the least."

"Indeed. Smart woman, you will excel fast in this world yet." The music ended and everyone returned to their seats.

"Looks like James has caught a liking to you Angel." Eva looked around the table as everyone gapped at the comment Braxton had thrown at her. He must have forgotten that they were not alone, he never called her Angel publicly.

"Um…" Before she could get any words to come out the host drew everyone's attention to him. Sue leaned over.

"Angel? Since when does he calls you that?"

"I don't know be quiet will you." Eva glanced at Braxton from the corner of her eyes, he did not seem to notice the slip of his tongue, he was completely at ease. Eva could not miss the look Michelle Anderson was throwing at her. Eyes darker than the usual green she had.

The host continued his speech. "Thank you all for coming out tonight to celebrate Green Works. It has been a pleasure working with all the investors and of course, none of this would have been possible without the genius mind of Mr. Braxton Carter. Ladies and Gentlemen, please give him a round of applause." It seemed like everyone there knew who he was and right then Michelle clapped and brushed a kiss across his cheek. She saw his jaw muscles tighten.

"Now if you all can dig into your wallets, we will be sending an envelope around to each table please donate for a good cause and after we will start up the dance and clothes auctions." Eva could not hide her irritation from her voice as she spoke low to Braxton.

"Look at you Mr. Carter, seems like a certain Miss. Anderson is laying claim to you." Pausing.

"At least for tonight. Bravo to her. She is bold." He leaned over to her, brushing his lips discreetly across Eva's cheek.

"She is just a business associate, she is nobody." His sister chimed in, interrupting their private conversation.

"I've already listed our names in the auction we should make our way to the stage." Eva, unable to protest, was glaring at his sister. She stood next to her on stage.

"Eva, I hope you don't mind that I added your name, it is for a good cause, and besides if you want to win my brother you cannot do that being in the background."

"Melinda…"

"Linnie all my friends call me Linnie."

"Linnie I am not trying to win your brother. What you saw was a onetime thing we both understand that."

"Really! Is that why you both cannot keep your eyes off each other just look at him now." Eva turned and saw Braxton making his way towards the stage.

"It doesn't matter anyway, that Anderson woman has her claws so deep into him it leaves no room for me to interlude."

"They are ancient history." Eva was taken aback as she knew there was something else besides a casual business relationship. Sue was up first, the opening bid started out at

1000. One person yelled 1500, all the way up to 10,000. Kevin did not get out bided. She and Michelle were the last two left.

"Now we have the lovely Evangeline Brun, a recent graduate who majored in Victorian Literature and now will expand her love for old times to greener technologies. Who wants to dance with this exotic beauty? She's dressed in a magnificent shade of green. Remember, all proceeds will be going to the Green works Agriculture charity." Eva blushed again this time with the whole room looking. Braxton's eyes never left hers. She saw his eyes were turning from silver to smoky gray.

"Opening bid at 1,000." Someone went up to 5,000. It was James. Not another dance with him if only Kevin would have bid for her. Braxton quickly lifted his hand.

"5,500 do I hear 6,000, 6,000 do I hear 6,500, 10,000, uh oh gentleman the stakes are getting high. Twenty thousand do I hear 20,500, going once, going twice and 20,500 to Mr. Carter. Eva heard Michelle gasp in surprise, she wanted to shrink again or at least have a drink. Twenty thousand was too much. She is going to have to pretend to fall so he does not waste his money.

The music was starting up again and they were being led to their proper dance partners by the staff. Eva walked to stand in front of Braxton. The passion in his eyes palpable to all those around them. He encircled her body in his arms much closer than he was when he was dancing with Michelle. Even closer than the first time they danced the night of the ball.

"Braxton, I told you I would dance with you, you should not have wasted so much money."

"Angel it is not a waste of money seeing how it will be going to research projects. He tipped her chin to look at him.

"Don't overthink it's for a good cause. Dancing with you is a bonus." He smiled down at her.

"You could have bid on other women." He leaned down lips touching her ear.

"I didn't want other women." She was breathing heavily now and mentally disturbed all at once.

"No, you are wrong if you wanted me, you would not have waited a month and a half to do something." He smiled.
What was funny?

"Angel I love your hair, reminds me of the one who sings "Touch Me in the Morning."

He is good, way to maneuver around the conversation. That's fine two can play the game he is playing, she is not innocent anymore.

"Braxton why don't we get out of here!" He looked shocked. *Good.*

"Of course, we could go to a hotel suite, it seems like you don't usually entertain in your own home." Eva felt him harden beneath her.

"Be careful what you ask for Angel, if you are not ready to play this game, I suggest you quit while you're ahead."

"Oh, I am ahead." They whirled in harmony with one another, not noticing the stilled dancers or the hushed tones. When the music ended, there was an eruption of applause as they ended the last steps of the waltz.

"Braxton that was embarrassing, I always seem to embarrass myself in your presence." She gave him a nervous laugh and her most seductive smile.

"That Angel was an amazing dance that people appreciated." Braxton never took his seat but strolled through the party talking to one person then another.

"Eva I did not realize you could dance like that, you two looked so perfect together." Sue praised her and Michelle sat down sour-faced. "Do you recall when I came home all the time complaining about the ballroom requirement? It was annoying, but I'm glad I did it." She winked at Sue and moved her eyes towards the frown on Michelle's face. Linnie's appraisal did nothing to help.

"Eva, oh, Angel I mean…You must teach me to dance like that, Braxton never mentioned you were a good dancer as well."

Eva knew she was doing all this to aggravate Michelle Anderson. Not wanting to be left out of the awkward conversation, she added, "Yes Evangeline." She pronounced each syllable.

"You are a great dancer. From all the functions I went to with Braxton I have never seen one to keep up with him like I could except tonight." She said those things to let Eva know she was staking her claim on him. Eva's phone buzzed again.

"Eva, who keeps on bothering you I saw you with that thing all night." Sue said.

"Oh, it's Jason, I think he is bored working at a gallery function tonight."

Meet me outside in five minutes.
B. Carter

I guess you booked a room already huh? That was fast. Anxious much…do better than the last time… it was really bad :(
Eva

Here I thought you would sign as Angel…I can assure you that this will not be bad. And the room in question is always ready.

P.S. It was not "BAD" last time. We had a different situation.
B. Carter

Well, what did she expect, she already knew him to be a modern-day Don Juan. It is better that they lay all the cards on the table.

"Sue My head is killing me, I think I am going to take off." She spoke to the remaining people at the table.

"It really was nice meeting everyone and nice to see you again Linnie." She responded.

"I'm sure I will see you around soon." Linnie winked at her as she hugged Susan and started towards the door.

What was she doing? Eva thought as she made her way across the crowded room.

Was she really going to make a preposition to Braxton that she would be his lover and friend? No Strings! Braxton was waiting in his car. A grand sport Veyron 16.4 Bugatti.

Oh, Wow! He held the passenger door open for her. She watched him ease in next to her.

"Very nice car, Braxton." He did not say anything but drove for a couple of minutes and pulled over. Maybe he was having second thoughts. He leaned over grabbing a fist full of her hair and kissed her senselessly. She was already feeling the pool of wetness between her legs.

"I have been waiting to do that all night." Braxton breathed out. She looked at him heavy breathing, chest rising and falling fast.

"I'm glad." She was dazed, hot, and bothered. They sat in silence as he sped down towards their destination. She wondered what hotel they would go to. Suddenly, she felt cheap that all her morals were just slowly fading away. Starting from being auctioned like cattle. A real-life coquette.

Chapter Twenty-Nine:

Braxton

They pulled up to his penthouse. It was eerily quiet and Eva was starting to get nervous. Especially after realizing this was not normal for him to entertain at his home.

"Did you forget something?" She asked, completely bewildered.

"No, I don't think so." His eyes held a bit of amusement.

Braxton quickly opened the door for her and ushered her to the elevators, neither speaking. He knew he was breaking all his rules. First having slept with a virgin and bringing a woman to his home. He just could not see himself treating her like his other lovers. She was growing on him more than he would have liked. As soon as the elevator stopped at his floor, before he could change his mind, he picked her up almost running to his room. She laughed. He missed that.

"Braxton, we do not have to do this here." She was giving him a chance to change his mind. He sat her on his bed taking her heels off one by one and kissing his way up her leg.

Climbing on top of her and running kisses along her nose and finally her mouth. *Slowly.* He thought. This time he will do this right. Their tongues melted together, he was pressing his body into hers. Not seeming to get close enough. Braxton slipped off her clothes without their kiss ever breaking. He found her wet and groaned.

"Angel you are always ready for me." He slipped one finger into her tight spot then another while she muffled her sighs.

"I don't want you holding back Angel, or I will stop." A threat he likely would not carry out.

"Please don't stop... please...please." She was grinding against his hand. He moved down to her wet spot and ran his tongue over her. She came grabbing his hair and pumping her hips to meet his mouth. She tasted good. He rose and grabbed a condom from his nightstand, even though he wanted the pureness of their union.

Eva felt like she was high. Her mind was cloudy, she missed this man. Being a sex friend will be harder than she anticipated. Opening the condom, he rolled it on to himself. She wanted to taste him as he did her but was scared she would not do it right. She would have to ask Sue about the etiquette of *Dick Sucking,* she giggled to herself.

"Is something amusing Angel?" He came down kissing her breast and teasing the other with his hand. She moaned.

"N... ooo." She wondered if it would hurt her again, she wanted to ask, but the moment could be spoiled as his tip grazed her entrance, she lay still squeezing her eyes shut.

"Angel look at me." She peered through half-close lids.

"I know I hurt you before, I know now, and I promise to never hurt you again." She nodded, relaxing a little bit. She wove her arms around his neck bringing his face to hers letting him know that she trusted him. He eased into her slowly, she felt her body adjust to his size and ever so slowly he began to move. An ache growing again at the apex of her thighs. She was moaning uncontrollably kissing his eyes, his nose, his lips, to his neck, back to his lips. He liked that she noticed. Before long, she was meeting his thrust with one of her own. He pulled out quickly.

"Is something wrong? Am I doing this wrong? He bit down on his lips before slowly entering her again.

"You are great Angel, it makes me wonder if you had some practice."

He said through gritted teeth. "No, I did not."

"I know, Angel, you are fit for me." With that, he kissed her again and put a hand to rub her clit. As she was on the verge of climaxing again, she wrapped her legs around his waist and he started pumping harder and harder until they climaxed in unison. Crying out her name.

Eva lay beside Braxton, their bodies together, he was spooning her. She wiggled a little bit.

"Angel if you keep doing that, I'm going to turn you on your stomach." She gasped and he chuckled.

"Brax that was really good, a true nightcap." She heard a tear and knew that this was about to be round two. She felt herself getting wet in anticipation for him again. He turned her to her back, kissed her, and rubbed his hands all over her body. She knew one place he needed to touch, or she was going to scream. Then he was there, two fingers slipping into her.

He whispered, "That round was for you, this one is for me." It sounded so bad but made her tighten herself around his fingers. He told her to turn on her stomach and get on her knees.

Grabbing a fistful of her hair he told her he was going to fuck her now. As he said that, he put the full length of him deep inside her. At first, it was painful but as she pumped back, and he forward she was climaxing before she knew it. Braxton knew he should not push her but he needed to fuck her like crazy. Hell, he felt crazy. He gave her all he had. She climaxed again calling his name and biting down on the pillow.

He was holding on to his wanting to savor this moment to make sure tomorrow she would feel and remember that it was him giving her all this pleasure. Slapping her on her ass, he felt her getting wetter and he came hard pulling her hair and grabbing the headboard. He eased out of her going to the bathroom to get a warm towel so he could put it between her legs. When he came back into the room, she had already put on her lacy underwear and was putting on her bra.

"What are you doing Angel?"

"I just assumed I would be going home now."

"I'm not done with you yet" He pulled her back down on his bed towel placed between her legs.

"That feels good, I think I'm going to be sore tomorrow."

"That's the plan Angel." He moved to lay beside her cradling her body in between his, where she belonged.

Before Eva drifted off into exhaustion she wanted to, no need to tell him how this was going to work. If she said it, it would take the sting off the words that she knew he was going to say eventually. She turned towards him kissing him lightly on the lips.

"Braxton, I just wanted to tell you that this thing we just did was great but…" He cut her off.

"Are you dumping me Angel?" To dump him they had to be together in the first place.

"I just want you to know that if you want to continue this, I do not want money, gifts, or vacations. Just sex with no strings attached…OK" She hoped she sounded more confident than she felt. He looked at the ceiling as if pondering her preposition.

"Oh, and I don't want anyone to know about this either, not Kevin and not your sister either."

"See Angel the problem with you is that you over analyze everything. How about no money or vacations as you say but dinner…come now, this is sure to work up an appetite." She pursed her lips.

"Fine and no gifts either, I'm not one of your lovers. I'm your friend." Penny clapped her hands. *Good job, I am proud.* He laughed and pulled her close.

"Whatever you say Angel."

Chapter Thirty:

Evangeline

Thunder roared its ugly head causing my breath to come in heap, I am shaking uncontrollably in the corner of a small confound space. I hear screams and smell blood as the thunder is continuously calling. I feel someone taking my hand and thrusting a locket in it and putting me inside a crate. I look up and it's my mama, my mother. I open my eyes wider as she closes the lid and I wail, and I wail and then nothing just the sound of thunder and a light right beside my ear.

It was a horrible smell, my noise burned with fumes unknown to me. I slowly opened the crate clutching the locket my mama gave me. I put it around my neck. Slowly I stood looking around the small, boxed home. There she was laying open-eyed, staring at the ceiling, bleeding so much that her hair matted to her face. I shook her calling her name she would not move. Mama, I cried repeatedly. A hand grabbed me from behind and I screamed.

The eyes blue like a burning flame. He slapped me once. "Where is it?" He was speaking in a language unknown to me. He slapped me again. Where's the fucking key you little peasant... Où at-elle mis...where did she put it? I could only stare as tears rolled down my face. He was hitting me over and over. I could taste blood in my mouth. I wanted to wake my mother up and run behind her so she could protect me. I did not touch the locket, maybe that was what he was after. Je ne sais pas quoi que ce soit. Laissez-moi tranquille! I repeated over and over.

"Angel, Angel, wake up!" Braxton shook her. She opened her eyes tears flowing freely down her face. She could not even begin to feel humiliated at the things she must have said. This time Braxton did not question her, he simply held her in his arms until the tears dried up. She looked at the clock on his nightstand it read 5:45 a.m. Too embarrassed to look into Braxton's eyes she nuzzled her head in the fuzz on his chest.

"Thank you, Braxton, I know what you must think of me." He tilted her head up to meet his gaze.

"Angel, I'm worried about you, will you talk to me…please." She almost wanted to share her most shocking secret with him.

"I cannot Braxton, I'm sorry." She thought he was going to let this go and as they both lay back down he cuddled her to his body. He started speaking from a distant memory.

"I was about ten years old when I saw my mother murdered." He stopped. She did not want him to continue but she snuggled closer.

"I was coming home from boarding school for vacation, and my father was entertaining one of his mistresses, a well-known fact to my mother. It was late when I arrived at our estate in Scotland. I was so excited to see my mum that I ran upstairs to her quarters. I wanted to surprise her. I crept into her sitting room through a false panel that leads into her room closet. I heard her begging for her life as a man stood over her with a knife. I was shocked, I could not move, and I could not speak." His voice had gone raspy. Eva turned towards him and he did not stir his eyes closed tightly.

"The man said nothing as he stabbed her over and over and stood watching her bleed out. I muffled a cry in my sleeve, too scared to do anything. After what seemed like hours of him staying there and life finally slipping from her, he left the room. I walked over to her and called her name softly. I remembered we had an alarm, and I pushed the panic button. My mum was my savior from my father's brutal beatings. That night was the last night that I cried it has been twenty-one years and I have not let a single tear slip from my eyes."

Her face was streaking with tears, as she now understood his detachment from women and overbearing of his sister. He saw the first woman he loved heinously murdered before his eyes. She felt a different connection to him. Right then it was not just sexual anymore. And if she thought that she was falling in love with him before, she was sure of it now.

"Braxton, I don't know what to say your mother was taken from you at an early age, but you cannot blame yourself had you come out you would not be here today." He wiped the tears that did not seem to stop flowing from her eyes.

"Angel, I have never told anyone that, not my therapist and not even the detectives when they questioned me about what happened. I could not. I told you because I trust you and you may not think it is helpful to talk about whatever it is that haunts your dreams and makes you fluent in French, but it's important to talk to someone. I did not realize that until tonight when you were screaming and crying in your sleep." He paused, kissing her lightly on her lips.

"I'm here for you Angel and I would never do anything to hurt you again, ever." She knew she could trust him before his revelation.

"Do you think you could get me water?"
He rose and went to the kitchen bringing her a bottle of water. She took a long swallow.

"I have been seeing a therapist for the last year and a half. Every month or so we meet up and talk about things." Braxton understood what she said to the therapist was confidential, he did not bother with questions, and he wanted her to be comfortable. He could tell this was hard on her.

"When I was sixteen, so about four…no almost five years ago I started having these vivid dreams. At first they were only at night and then they grew worse. They were coming even if I was napping and sometimes daydreaming. It was so frightening that I went weeks with little or no sleep at all. Until finally the director of the orphanage called a doctor and he prescribed me sleeping pills. At first, it seemed to work. So, I stopped taking them. I ended up close to where Sue and I currently live and received a scholarship for school, and I met and moved in with her." He stared at her, her eyes blank as if she was remembering a tortured part of her past.

"About the time I started seeing the therapist my dreams started again, she wanted me to try to remember them to write them down in a diary of sorts. I did that for a while too, but I gave that up. She recommended a medication called Ambien. I take them every evening at the same time, and it eliminates my dreams." She smiled.

"Only, I still dreamt of you sometimes." He thought she was speaking metaphorically, they had only met four months ago.

"Sue knows about my dreams, sometimes like last night I forget to take the pill and this is what happens."

"You said I was speaking French?" He nodded.

"Did you take French in school?" She looked perplexed.

"No, I cannot recall even learning French in my time at the orphanage." Now he was curious.

"Your parents gave you up for adoption?"

"I guess this is a mystery. I cannot seem to remember anything prior to coming to the orphanage when I was seven. My therapist says that my dreams are memories that I somehow blocked."

"So, in my dreams I…I…I…" He could tell she was not ready to talk about it.

"It's OK Angel you do not have to speak about it right now, whenever you are ready just know that I will be here when you need me." With a possessive arm, he pulled her in close to him. She wiggled to adjust herself.

"Angel if you move again, I will have to make love to you again." They made love again and he watched her sleep with no nightmares.

Chapter Thirty-One:

Braxton

Braxton got out of bed after watching Angel sleep, he wanted to do something special for her. Last night's revelation brought him closer to her. He wanted her to trust him, he wanted to be her only lover and she his. He called his assistant Tracy to make sure his yacht was set up for his arrival later.

Eva came around, wrapping her arms around his waist. "Good morning handsome."

"It is a good morning Angel." Braxton placed a soft kiss on her lips.

"I hope you do not have plans for the day I want to take you somewhere." Eva grabbed a cup of coffee and a bagel, feeling famished after all that sex.

"No, no plans Braxton, I was going to meet up with Jason tonight, but I can cancel." He remembers the guy from the ball and the club that night. He felt a tinge of jealousy.

"Jason…who is that?" He came out right and said that.

"He is a friend of mine from school."

She paused, adding, "Not a friend like you."

"He isn't?" Braxton said more as a question as he picked her up and sat her on the countertop, kissing her with all the possessiveness he could muster. He heard someone behind him clear their throat.

"Linnie, as always, you are here at an inopportune time, please give Eva the bag you picked up at her apartment. If you will excuse me ladies, I have something to take care of."

Eva hopped off the counter, glancing shyly at his retreating back and the knowing glance of his sister. "Eva, you really put a spell on my brother, I have not seen him this happy in my whole twenty-one years." Linnie fixed herself with a cup of coffee. "Linnie, your brother and I are just friends."

"I know my brother has major commitment issues, but I can tell you are good for him." Penny's heart was pounding. *Opening up to him, he is the one I could feel it.*

"We will see Linnie and thanks for last night." Linnie smiled at her as Eva left to go and shower her aching body.

■■■

Chapter Thirty-Two:

Evangeline

She went into Braxton's room and pulled out the clothes Sue packed for her, which of course was not hers. She added a small pink cotton dress with studded sandals and no underwear. She was going to kill her. As she was finishing putting on her clothes his housekeeper came in with a note.

Angel, go to this address my driver will be waiting for you in the lobby, he will be your chauffeur for the day his name is Nathan. No arguments, I will be in a meeting until one.
B. Carter

It was only eleven. *What was he planning?* She was happy as can be as she strolled to get into the car parked out front waiting for her. "You must be Nathan, I'm Eva." She shook his hand, but he remained silent. Not the talkative type. They arrived at Luxe. A top-rated spa. She would have to talk to him about this, she recalled saying, "no gifts." As she walked in, a woman came and greeted her by name. "Miss. Brun we were expecting you, please follow me. We have you set up for a luxury two-hour spa package, if you need anything please do not hesitate to ask."

****

The two hours flew by too quickly and she felt so relaxed all the tenderness from their lovemaking gone. She felt like a new woman. The woman who greeted her before came and gave her another note. *So, this is a scavenger hunt sort of…interesting.*

Angel, I hope you enjoyed a bit of relaxation, I know you said no gifts, this is my way of making sure you will be able to keep up tonight, your next destination is on the back and remember that I said no arguing. I cannot wait to see you and see how flexible you are now that you are loose.

B. Carter

She could not keep the smile from her face as she flopped down in the back seat of his car. She had to call Sue.

"Sue, oh my gosh! You would not believe what a day I have had." Eva heard moaning in the back.

"Sue...Sue." She must have accidentally answered the phone. She decided to text Braxton for some playful banter.

Sorry Braxton, I would have hoped that you did not go overboard as I told you last night I did not want any of these things!

Eva

Are you angry? I can call everything off. Although I put in a lot of work for today.

B. Carter

Jeez, she did not want him to think she was ungrateful, he could not take a joke.

Mr. Handsome I was not being serious, but in the future let's tone it down a little.

Angel

He did not text her back. They were driving for almost an hour and her stomach let out a growl.

"Hey Nathan, can we stop by to pick up a pizza or something." She didn't think he was going to answer her.

"Miss. Brun, we have a strict schedule to stay on, I will see what I can get for you." They arrived at a boutique in the Hamptons. She had never been on this side of New York before.

As she walked, a young brunette came up to her with a note. "You must be Miss. Brun, we have heard so much about you." She shook the woman's hand and took the note.

"Nice to meet you, so what exactly am I doing here today?"

"I will personally be assisting you with picking out a dinner dress and next door is a salon. I believe you are going there next. I was just told to give you the note and ensure you do not leave without a proper dress. By the way, my name is Thea." Eva shook her head, whatever Braxton was planning was getting her anxious. She was no longer worried about the extravagance as to the mystery of the hunt she was on. She unfolded his note, excitement building in her.

Angel, first I want to say thank you for your patience. I, myself find a liking to William Shakespeare as he said "How poor are they that have no patience!" What wound did it ever heal but by degrees?" I'm burning for you. You have one final stop before joining me. If you could take some advice I love the soft colors on you, it blends well with the honey-kissed skin you have.

Awaiting your company

B. Carter

Eva got emotional as she read and reread his note. She wondered how many women he had done this for or was she the first. They had her try on almost two dozen dresses. An hour and a half later, she picked out a Jovani beige cocktail dress with a beaded waistline. Thea informed her that after the she left the salon to return to put the dress on.

At the salon next door Eva did not even worry about her rumbling stomach, she told the stylist to put her hair in messy tiny spirals the way that Braxton loved.

Apparently, she was to have her make-up done as well, she wanted to do something exotic and different than the norm she always did. She allowed the make-up artist to do a smoky eyed look with a hint of gold surrounding her eyes. After returning to put on the dress she snapped a picture and sent it to Sue, who called her within two minutes.

"Hey lover girl, I called you earlier while you were otherwise engaged." Eva said with a hint of amusement in her tone.

"Oh, sorry about that what's going on with you, I have so much to tell you."

Eva with excitement in her voice started sharing the events of her day. "Braxton has something planned out, and by the way you did not pack me underwear Sue, how subtle. I did not want everyone to know about his and I relationship. I guess he did not get that."

"It's OK, it's not like you could have hid it, when you both left minutes apart last night, anyway you look great I will see you tomorrow."

She hung up the phone as she was ushered into the waiting car.

■■■

■■

Eva must have dosed off, she was being awakened by the coughs of Nathan. "Miss. Brun we have arrived if you would accompany me I will take you to Mr. Carter's yacht."

His what. Penny did a dive into the water. She looked around and noticed that there were a lot of people moving about. As they were walking, she was stopped abruptly by the sound of her name. She turned around and saw Michelle.

"Evangeline is that you?" She inhaled deeply, forcing a smile.

"Yes, how are you Michelle? What brings you out here today?" Eva noticed that she looked her up and down.

"Why I could ask you the same thing? I was visiting a friend here today, but now I must take my leave. It was a pleasure seeing you again so soon." Before Eva could respond, Michelle left her standing looking dumbfounded. *Was she there with Braxton? He would not, would he?* She and Nathan walked to the docks until she was standing next to a vast yacht with the name Bella scrolled against its body.

She walked on the ship and saw how beautifully it was decorated. She could tell where Braxton's love for the green movement ventured into the designs of this yacht. As she glanced around admiring the details of the deck, she saw him as deliciously breathtaking. He had on a crisp white linen top and slacks with a few buttons open at the chest. She could see why all the women flocked to him. He walked towards her, taking her hand and kissing her knuckles.

"How are you Angel?" *Crap! No word Lucy will be her new name.* She could not think of a word to say.

"I hope you did not mind the goose chase you were on." He led her to the back of the yacht where there was a private canopy tent sat up with pillows surrounding the invisible walls. In the middle was a floor table with different varieties of fruits.

"Thank you for everything today, it was almost like my regular routine." She winked. "And even a little fun. Although I have to say Nathan may have literally said less than ten words to me in the last several hours."

Laughingly he said, "Yes Nate is not one for talking, which is why I asked him to do this today. I did not want you making nice with other men." He grinned devilishly.

"Jealous?"

"Never, it's a man thing." They sat as she noticed the ship was slowly sailing away.

"Who is driving?"

"That would be Nate, he has many talents I could not began to say."

"Except for polite conversation, you know it was really weird riding with him."

He picked up a fruit that she had never seen before in her life. "Here try this."

He put it in her mouth. "Mmmm…very sweet." He wiped the trail of juice from her mouth with his finger.

"I am going to admit, I am ignorant as to what this is."

"It is called Rambutan native in Southeast Asia. I have them imported. My mother used to make jam sandwiches from these when I was a kid."

"Is the boat named after her?" His eyes were saddened.

"Yes, Isabella was her name." They sat alone in silence for moments until they finally stood, taking her hand and standing behind her as they led them to the rear to overlook the retreating shoreline.

"Braxton it seems like every time I am with you words elude me, and I find it very difficult to talk to you with you being in such close proximity."

Braxton did not know what it was that made him do the craziest things when it came to her. He wants her to trust him and for them to build a friendship. It was easy being himself whenever he was with her. When he saw her come on his boat, he all but carried her to his cabin. He wanted to connect with her to possess her more than he wanted anything in his life. It was not love, it was him seeing something he wanted and would stop at nothing to get it.

"Angel, you can be yourself when you are with me, why do I make you short for words?" He turned her around, nuzzling at her nape.

"Well for starters it has something to do with what you are doing now." He felt her pulse quicken as his lips grazed the vein on the side of her neck.

"Also, that you seem to be leading Michelle on." He stopped her.

"Michelle?" What the hell does she have to do with this?"

"She said in not so many words that she was here with you all day."

"Eva, she and I are ancient history. And yes, she did come today to sign over some documents I needed for her former company." He kissed her softly on her lips, letting his tongue find the words that he could not.

"Eva, you must understand that she means nothing to me, but you…you are starting to mean a great deal more than I expected. Let us go to the dining room. I believe the dinner is ready. Nate said that you were begging for food all day." He thumped her on the nose. She punched him in the arm.

"I was not begging, but after last night, and only having a bagel I was expected to be hungry after several hours, sir." He had a chef come and make a light dinner. Sushi, Filet Mignon

with twice-baked potato accompanied with béarnaise sauce

drizzled on top of asparagus. For dessert, a simple selection of

hazelnuts and fruit Pavlova.

"Braxton everything looks great." He uncovered all the

dishes except one that held a surprise for her.

"What is under that one?"

"You will find out soon enough."

They were talking about his plans for a new startup

company. She told him how she was going to finish her major in

environmental science the following year.

"You can always come work for me Angel."

"No, I did that before."

He looked confused. "Care to elaborate."

"No, I would much rather do something else." He pulled

her into his lap, moving his hands up her dress.

"You seem to be missing an essential part of your

attire."

"Yes Sue." She stopped as he uncovered the last lid with her underwear folded neatly on the tray. "Braxton, between you and Sue I do not know which one of you is worse." He laughed.

"I was wondering if you were going to take another pair of my shorts again, I am glad you proved me wrong."

To her disappointment, he did not carry on touching her. Instead, he led her to his cabin, and they lay together spooning. "Angel, I know you are not willing to talk about what happened this morning, but I brought you here because I think that you need to make a decision."

She turned around sitting on top of him. If she could distract him, maybe he would drop this whole thing. She started kissing he neck and unbuttoning his shirt. "I know what you are trying to do and believe me as I am sure you can tell it is working for half of me, but." She bit his lip.

"Alright that's it."

■■■

They made love as the sunset. Eva tired from running around all day. She did not want to bring up that it may be time to leave.

Eva did not take her medication and as most times memories of her childhood would break a peaceful night.

"Braxton, as much as I would love to stay and sleep here with you I think that it is time for us to leave."

"On the contrary Angel, we will be staying the night here."

"Braxton you know why I cannot stay."

"Angel trust me, I have your medication and it will be your choice if you take it or not. I do believe that from the memory lapse that you have had, your dreams are exactly that. Memories that you are shoving away, if you really want to remember what happened to you then I think you should embrace your dreams. You are older now, don't let them scare you. I will be right here next to you."

What was she going to do? Penny interjected, *I know, stop taking the pills your mother was murdered don't you want to remember why? Where is the locket? The mugging outside the club, the French words spoken to you. Honor her memory. Consciously it all made sense, hell for that matter Braxton did too.*

"OK, but don't freak out. I feel so abnormal, and I hate for Sue to see me like that, what makes you think I will feel any different about you."

"Angel, if we are to be friends, then let me be your friend." He went and started a fire in the fireplace and Eva stared into the flames laying horizontally on the bed.

Oh, Madame where are you taking me, where is my mother? I looked around as a stout African woman was taking me away. I knew this was not my mother. I recalled seeing her thrusting a locket in my hands from a past moment or a later memory. Where was she taking me? Your mother asked me to take you somewhere safe, Amoureux. I heard a big bang and my safe keeper took me to a tent set out for the servants down river. Why is everyone fighting Madame? I started shaking and in the distance I heard someone say, "Angel it is OK I'm here'. Is Braxton the love of my life here? He's in danger, I have to find him, I must be calm, I trip, I fall and memories every sordid one came crushing against my skull.

"Angel wake up its time for us to go. I have some clothes for you in the bathroom." He kissed her on her forehead.

"That was the best sleep I have had in a long time Braxton." She had another dream but this time she was calm and obviously did not disturb Braxton. Should she tell him about her dream? No, the memories were too painful. She knew what she needed to do. Find her mother's locket with the key and go to France and start at the beginning.

Chapter Thirty-Three:

Evangeline

September rolled in and Eva was able to be hired at Go Go Green Technology Inc. It was a startup company, and she had an entry level position as an Administrative Assistant to the CEOs Senior Administrator. This was her break she spent a couple months trying to get a position or an internship but without the proper qualifications no one was willing to hire her. Eva started taking more science classes at NYU. Eva, only twenty-one, had plenty of time to major in another discipline. Although she managed to keep her feelings for Braxton under his nose, they spent a lot of time together getting to know one another. When Eva came home after another charity function, she saw Sue and Kevin huddled together on their sofa.

At the end of the night, he apparently decided to take her to Lady Liberty herself and proposed. She was truly happy for her friend. Sue was finally at a place in her life where she would have her happily ever after.

Sue barged into her room "Hey Eva my pre-engagement party is in a couple days. Do you want to go shopping? Kevin gave me his credit card and told me to go to Neiman Marcus!" All she wanted to do was sit and relax. It was a long strenuous day at work.

"Sue I'm really tired and there is a meeting in a couple days at my job and I have to prepare. This is the day where the big CEO is going to finally make an appearance." She did not notice the bag Sue was holding until she started swinging it in her hand.

"Yea, I figured you would say that, you have been saying that a lot lately. You are too tired to do this and Miss. I cannot go to that bar and do that…jeez what do you and Braxton do when you're together, I'm surprised you have the energy to wear those SEXY things you think you hid in your closet."

Eva felt herself flush. She felt guilty, she was always working, sleeping, or with Braxton. She was being a horrid best friend and she knew it.

"I'm really sorry Sue, let's go have some coffee at Roger's and we can catch up. It's just that work has really been kicking my butt lately." Sue glanced at her, rolled her eyes, and sat down next to her on the bed. She shoved the bag at her. It was from the pharmacy. She peered inside smiling, knowing Sue she was bound to give her a box of condoms.

"Eva you know I love you like my very own sister."

"Sue you do not have a sister."

"That is beside the point, had I a sister in another life you would be her and besides you are the closet I have in that department." Eva pulled out three pregnancy tests all top of line. One was the five days in advance and the other two were electronic: Yes and Nos.

"Sue are you pregnant?" Sue grabbed her hand.

"No honey I'm not, I'm on the pill which will be rectified as soon as I am Mrs. Kevin Smith-Dole." She put her hand through my hair. "I bought these for you.

Eva jumped up. "Me, Me, why the hell would you do that! For the love of God, we use C-O-N-D-O-M-S!" She spelled the word out as if talking to a child.

"Honey OK I'm sorry I'm not questioning, nor do I need details on how you two get it on, but did you use condoms every time, even still you know they could break." Eva felt like she was getting the safe sex talk from a mother.

"Ye...yes... we did." She paused.

"Shit not first time, but it lasted literally ten seconds, I told you that. Surely not then, he didn't even orgasm I think."

"Be that as it may, I bought these because I've had my period twice now being the second. And you haven't had it once and we have them at the same time." Eva closed her eyes, her fears bubbling up at the surface. She prayed this was not true, Braxton would leave her and worse he would tell her to get an abortion.

"We will deal with this, don't worry. Kevin brought it up the night of the charity function."

"Kevin! He will tell Braxton for sure, maybe he did tell him, he has been distant lately."

"No Eva don't worry he will not. I told him it is not his place." Eva grabbed Sue's hand, her room feeling much smaller than it was.

"Let's go in on the bathroom I will be there with you. If it is positive you have some things that you will have to discuss with Braxton and this decision, whatever you decide will be yours…" She stopped.

"And I will be here with you every step of the way. Hell, when I move out after I'm married you could live here it's paid off whether you keep the baby or not you will live here."

Tears sprang to Eva's eyes. She was condemned and knew before she took the test it would be positive. She reflected on the last few months when she thought she had the flu. And medicine, tea, nor soup would help her stop vomiting.

Her sense of certain smells was a distant reminder. If she ever thought she was in hell, this was surely it. They both walked to the bathroom and Sue produced a cup. She just sat on the floor a while wanting this to be a dream. This was worse than any of her nightmares. She'd become a true statistic.

"Eva go ahead let's get this over with. If you were stressed out as you were saying, your cycle could have been affected."

Eva understood she was only saying this to ease her discomfort, they both knew that she was pregnant. She flopped down on the toilet and put her urine in the cup. She unwrapped the first box, not the fancy ones, the good old-fashioned plus and minus. She gave one to Sue, she took the other, and together they both dipped the stick and sat it on the counter. Waiting.

"We could go and have some tea and come back later to look." Sue suggested.

Putting on a false bravado that she did not feel in the least, Eva said, "No, let's just get this over with, it's not like it's the end of the world, right?"

"No honey it is not." After two minutes they both picked up the sticks. A big pink plus appeared on both of theirs.

"NO, NO, NO!" Eva chanted for how long she did not know. Sue grabbed her by the waist before she could sink to the ground and they went into the living room. Tears cascading down her cheeks, uncontrollably soaking her clothes. "Shh, shh, it's OK Eva, I'm here you are not alone, you have me and Kevin." Eva felt a hot cup being thrust in her hands as she looked up to stare at Kevin's face. *When did he get there?*

She saw pity in his eyes. He knew, as did she, Braxton would take her to the clinic immediately, no questions asked. She looked deeper into his eyes, pleading with him on her own.

"You cannot tell him please, I will." She whispered. Sue and Kevin went to the kitchen and talked. Her phone vibrated.

Hey, how are things going at work? Not working too hard...

B. Carter

What was she going to say, *work is fine but I am having your baby.*

Work is work...

Eva

Is something wrong?

B. Carter

He must have a sixth sense for this stuff, he always seemed to be there when she was falling apart. New tears came to her eyes, at the loss of either, a silver eyed baby boy with dimples. Or the loss of the silver-eyed man who set her soul on fire, the man who made her feel precious and beautiful despite her ethnicity and the shame society wanted her so badly to feel.

Angel? I am worried...I am coming over are you home?

B. Carter

She could not have him come, her eyes red rimmed from crying half an hour straight.

No, I am fine. I must have dozed off. Between you and work, I do not really sleep often.

Eva

Are you coming for drinks tonight? I have an announcement.

B. Carter

Sure, I will come.

Eva

Ok, I will see you later, I can send Nathan to pick you up...sounds good.

B. Carter

No, I will come with Kevin and Sue

Eva

See you later Angel

B. Carter

She would get through this already, deciding that she would in no way kill a child that was growing inside her. She put a possessive hand on her stomach. She knew she was going to be alone in this with the exception of Sue and Kevin. Eva would put on her big girl panties, be a woman and to hell with Braxton if he wanted no part in this then, *oh well, his loss!*

Chapter Thirty-Four:

Evangeline

They arrived at a lovely French restaurant: Le Bernadin. This was Eva's first time at a restaurant like this. She put on a soft pink lace cap-sleeve cocktail dress that Braxton sent over with Nathan that night, despite her telling him an hour ago that she would go with Sue and Kevin. Adding to that, the gifts he sent which always had a reason for why she needed them. This pink dress was a congratulatory gift for getting a job. He was smart enough to remove the price tag, but Sue saw the name Oscar de la Renta and sighed. Eva did not know what that meant.

They sat down in the private dining area. It was decorated in bamboo woods on the ceiling and floor. And ivory silk tablecloths. White hydrangeas filled the room with their sweet smell and sat atop all the tables in a crystal vase. She was glad he did send over the dress, nothing in her closet would be OK wearing to a place like this. Kevin, Sue, and Eva sat at the long elegantly decorated table that could easily sit twelve people.

"How many people are coming here?" Sue shrugged her shoulders. Just then Braxton came in with his sister Linnie, along with Michelle as well as several other men and women. They all stood to exchange handshakes with Kevin while Eva stood in the background. Linnie came over to her.

"Wow Eva you look so beautiful in that dress, I wanted to get you black, but Braxton insisted that with your tone you should wear a soft pink and he was right." Linnie had on the same dress instead, hers was a scarlet red. She could see Michelle standing close to Braxton's hand on his arm. She rolled her eyes.

"What is it with her? She is so desperate." Linnie turned around.

"She is desperate and thinks she will rekindle something between her and my brother. She is like fatal attraction that one."

They all took their seats with Braxton sitting next to her and before Michelle was able to sit on his right his sister shooed her away. She had on a long black gown with her hair in a mess of curls. Eva smiled to herself, she tried to mirror Eva's natural hair, she looked terrible. Eva, for one, was glad she had her hair in loose spirals. Eva would have hated even having a resemblance to that wicked woman. Braxton pulled out his sister's chair then turned his eyes to her, smiling until he looked into hers. He pulled her chair out a kissed her cheek. He whispered in her ear.

"I thought you said you were fine. Your eyes are rimmed in red." Before she could respond, the waiter came to take their orders. He came around to her. She recalled her memories when she was speaking French.

"Mademoiselle… Mademoiselle… Mademoiselle, que voulez-vous? What would you like?" He was French as well. She looked and saw Michelle snickering at her, seeing how she did not have a clue what she was going to order. Michelle spoke.

"Maybe you should explain to her what is on the menu."

She whispered something to the man next to her and they giggled. She was flushed again not because of embarrassment but because of her strong dislike of this woman. Braxton was about to order for her when she stopped him.

She looked at the menu again and like an epiphany she could read and understand everything on there. Her secretly studying French with her tutor lately helped immensely.

Thankfully ordering was covered in the first few chapters.

"Monsieur, je vais avoir du saumon pour le premier cours, le thon albacore, de l'agneau et du homard pour le plat principal. Pas de vin pour moi, je viens de découvrir que j'étais enceinte." Her heart raced as she spoke her broken French. The waiter bowed leaving to retrieve the wine. He returned moments later pouring and skipping over hers with a wink. Everyone stared at her open mouthed. Michelle turned bright red, a replica of a she-devil in a black dress and red face. Eva smiled at her. Sue said.

"Eva, I didn't know your French had gotten so good, way to hold out on me! Just think of the men we could have seduced." She said winking to Kevin. Sue was the only other person who knew of Eva's tutoring. Instead of giving her the real reason, she told her it was a new hobby. One of the men asked her to teach him something, while another asked her where she was from. Braxton took her hand under the table and put it on his erection.

"I take it you remember those French lessons." He smirked at her.

"You just want me to talk dirty to you." She whispered and winked as another conversation started with the other guest.

After their final course, Eva was stuffed. She loved the food here. Before dessert arrived, Braxton stood requesting everyone's attention.

"I wanted everyone here tonight to celebrate the successful opening of another Green Work technology company and the successful purchase of Miss. Anderson's factories. On behalf of Carter Enterprise, we will be launching our green technology in various parts of western Africa to start. We have already gotten great feedback on our fish farm. We are hoping that this will bring awareness to freshwater sourcing..." He continued. Everyone clapped. Eva's heart melted if only she could be a part of this forever. She felt as if she was on the verge of tears as she rose up from her chair, Sue looking at her. She shook her head as Sue squeezed her hand. She walked out into a busy but quiet night in Manhattan. She had not taken her first breath before Braxton came to her, pulling her close. She cried again this time heavy tears dripped on his suit jacket. He tipped her chin up to him.

"What is going on Angel? I know something is wrong. Have you had more dreams like before? Are you starting to remember?" She shook her head in between gasps of air. She knew she was being dramatic.

"I...don't want to t-t-alk... about it. It will ruin your night." She took a deep breath, willing herself to regain a steady breathing pattern. People walked past them, turning their faces at them, trying to figure out if this was a lovers' quarrel.

"I told you I'm here for you, you can tell me anything. And if I have to worry about you all night that will ruin it, trust me. If you want, we can leave now." She shook her head unable to look into his eyes. She knew he didn't like public scenes. She had to kiss him one last time before she told him something that she knew would destroy everything they have. She pulled his jacket down and wrapped her hands around his neck. He looked around tentatively at the passersby. She turned his face towards hers.

"I care about you a lot and in another life maybe we could have been together differently than our current arrangement." He tried to speak. She silenced him with a soft kiss.

"I told you in the beginning from the first night I was in your arms you have no need to be committed to me, I'm a big girl." He smirked dimples at all.

"Angel are you breaking up with me?" It was a question he hid with a nervous laugh. How she would miss that.

"Braxton we were never together, silly." She kissed him softly pecks at first and then their kisses grew greedily, tongues swirling he grabbed and her face. When she tried to pull it back. He wrapped an arm around her waist, bringing her closer to him. He broke the kiss first, her lips immediately feeling his absence.

"Why do I get the feeling that was the last kiss?" She gave him a weak smile. Penny deciding now was the time to appear.

Tell him! He loves you! Look at the way his eyes are glistening with unshed tears. He will not leave you alone! Trust in him, trust in love. Eva let go, it is a time to love. She pushed those thoughts aside. She did not want to ruin the day he prepared his whole career for.

"We will still be friends count on it, but lovers I cannot be something that which I criticize." She turned to go hail a cab.

"Angel do not leave me...please." He was rubbing a finger over her jaw line.

"We can try but you have to understand why it's hard for me to have relationships. I feel like we have something special we can build on it slowly." He was pleading.

This was going to be harder than she anticipated, she assumed he would be OK, it is not like he said a declaration of love for her.

"Angel don't make me beg...I don't want you to go."

"Je t'ai aimé dès le premier moment que je t'ai vu. Nous ne pouvons pas être ensemble parce que je vais avoir votre bébé."

"Come on Angel what does that mean? That doesn't sound like dirty talk." He tried to lighten the atmosphere.

"Je suis enceinte... Je suis enceinte..." She turned around and left in the cab.

Chapter Thirty-Five:

Braxton

Braxton returned into the restaurant ready to say his goodbyes to everyone, so he could go get his Angel. He was not done with her just yet. He was saying the phrase she said over and over aloud *Je suis enceinte.* He did not understand French, and he was completely perplexed at how she suddenly picked the language. Before he could go into the private dining area, he was stopped by a tall dark-haired woman with red lips.

"Monsieur, j'espère que vous n'êtes pas enceinte!" She spoke with an accent. And there was that word again. E*nceinte.*

"Excuse me, I don't speak French." She batted her lashes.

"I assumed... your accent is very good, please pardon me Monsieur." He wanted to ask her what that meant. All eyes were on him as he grabbed her arm not too tight.

"What was I saying?" She smiled shyly.

"You were saying 'I'm pregnant.'" Braxton could not move, he stood rooted to the ground and panic quickly descended, his heart racing. He stormed through the private dining area. He went directly to Eva's empty chair.

"Sue, please tell me you know nothing about this?" He said in a hushed tone, although the room was quiet, his voice echoed.

"Not here." Was that all she said to him? He excused himself from the dinner and left his credit card with his sister. She asked him if everything was that all right.

"I'll talk to you later Linnie, it's Angel. I can't explain it now, but I will call you later or tomorrow." Michelle stood as if she wanted to say something. He gave her the look of 'Don't Fucking Talk.' She sat down immediately. He picked up his phone to call Nathan to pull the car around the front.

Braxton stood outside Eva's apartment wanting to talk to her. What did she think she was doing? She slept with him that very morning in his arms and all the while she was carrying some other man's baby. It did not make sense.

How? When? He was hurt and he realized in that moment he fell completely in love with her. He used protection with her every time. He needed to confront her and ask her why, why she would come to him make love to him, with him and leave to go to someone else's bed. He did the same thing this man did to him in the past and now he regrets every woman he trifled with. This feeling was unimaginable.

Is this how they felt? He pounded on the door and nothing. He texted her phone.

Angel Answer the fucking door now or I will break it down

B. Carter

Angel just tell me why you would do something like this to me, of all people. I was always up front with you. You lack the common courtesy to give me the same.

B. Carter

He sat in his car calling her phone and she started sending him voicemails.

Was she here? Or with the other man she was leaving him for? Would he be willing to raise another man's child? Was she getting an abortion? No, she wouldn't have mentioned to him. He texted her again.

> *Angel, are you trying to hurt me? I get it... but at least tell me why. I deserve that much.*

B. Carter

> *No Evangeline, I need to rephrase that. You did hurt me*

B. Carter

Chapter Thirty-Six:

Evangeline

Evangeline sat in her room staring down at Braxton as he paced in front of her apartment. Giving up he went into his car. He left several voice messages. She read his text messages over and over. He knew she was pregnant and he must have gotten that much out of their conversation. She bit back a choke, as she understood what he meant in his messages. He thought she had gotten pregnant purposefully and was doing this to torment him.

She wanted to explain that this was far from what she wanted. *Hell, he knew more about impregnating through intercourse than she did.* She wanted things to work between them, she had his baby growing in her. But she had to walk away before he told her to have an abortion. Eva wouldn't ask for anything, and to be sure they can make arrangements to keep it concealed and his rights given up as a parent.

With a heavy heart and battered soul, Eva took her pill and cried herself asleep.

A few days later Eva stirred in her sleep. It was nearing seven a.m. Today was the day of her best friend's engagement party and when the CEO of the company came for an introduction. She jumped out of bed not wanting to do anything but sleep and be miserable. She had to get her life back together. Braxton did not text or call after his explosion outside her apartment. *It was better this way.* She had to focus. By Eva's calculation she was three and a half months pregnant and had no prenatal care. Putting everything out of her mind she rose and went into her daily morning routine before work.

Eva got out of the taxi in front of her job in Brooklyn. She went straight to her desk and began to prepare the files for the meeting with the CEO and the staff. She gathered materials that she hoped would give her an edge in the meeting. Eva wanted an offer for a full-time position and not just a paper pusher. She scoped out their competitors and the products that they use and researched "how green each company claimed to be." It took most of the month and all of yesterday to finalize while she was abed. She needed something to get her mind off Braxton, their last kiss, and his last words to her. Tracy was, her supervisor and the private assistant to the CEO. She was the only one who knew who their mysterious leader was. She came and announced that the meeting was going to start in ten minutes and that everyone should be in the boardroom immediately. She walked to the boardroom anxiously waiting to meet the person who was promising to lead this company to the next generation of green technology. Eva sat pen in hand with a notepad every bit of a businesswoman. For today's introductory meeting all the employees under the management of Tracy sat around the large oval table. There were eleven total working in this sector. She did not know anyone personally, since being hired she made it her business like her other job to not befriend anyone.

Eva drifted back to the messages Braxton left, wanting to hear his voice again remembering its silkiness.

As if conjuring him up in her mind, he walked in commanding the room as his own. He sat at the head of the table. She was in shock. Instead of her usual cherry flush she sported, all the blood drained from her face. She was ghostly pale. He looked at her, his eyes not the normal silver but like grey oil. He looked at her stomach before snapping his gaze to his P.A. throwing commands. The woman on her left was what some may call a blonde Barbie.

She said to her friend, "Even in a bad temper he is sexy and that is Braxton Carter...I will give him the business as soon as possible." They giggled softly to themselves. Eva felt a strong surge of jealousy as the woman kept batting her long perfect lashes at him. He smiled at her with his dimple.

"Good Morning everyone, I do apologize for keeping everyone in suspense, it was necessary before the buyout was concluded. My plans here will be to run a tight ship. I know we all have our personal lives, but this company is a startup, and we need everyone to have their full attention on the upcoming projects. If anyone here is married, have children, or…" He looked at her again.

"Expect to have children then I suggest you prioritize

accordingly." He went on about new policies and contracts

that we all have to sign. As the meeting concluded, she saw

Barbie girl sway her hips towards him and talking softly.

She was sure it was an indecent proposal by the way

he winked at her as she was turning to leave. Eva was two

seconds away from fleeing or fighting for the man she

loved. She craved to make him understand that she did not

manipulate him into fathering a child she was not ready to

have. She was walking head down and collided into

Braxton's chest. She inhaled his scent, and her heart began

to beat in an unsteady rhythm. Eva quickly put her hand to

her stomach. To touch their growing baby.

This was the position they found themselves in right

before he used to take control of her body. She looked in

his eyes hoping to see something there. Something that will

assure her that he did not mean what he said. She saw only

one thing, hurt. He moved her aside and walked away without a word. Eva knew that at that moment he would never forgive her. Already deciding that she was going to put in a two-week notice. There was no way she could work for the father of her baby while he banged everything that had breast and an entrance.

She sat at her desk, the Barbie across from her was talking about how she was going to screw him as he never was before. Penny appeared.

Do not worry about her, you were the best he ever had, how many guys can get a girl pregnant in less than ten seconds. Eva rolled her eyes.

Tracy called her into her office.

"Good Morning Tracy, is there anything else I can do for you?"

Tracy smiled at her. She was always kind to her from the beginning. "Come in and shut the door."

Eva did as she was told and sat in a comfortable leather chair. Tracy's office was decorated in light neutral colors. Everything in the building was either recycled or made from renewable energies. Each window had the same window treatments that Braxton had shown her in his penthouse. "It was brought to my attention that you are expecting a baby…is that correct?"

She was on the verge of tears. *How dare Braxton tell people about her. And furthermore, what the hell does a baby have to do with this.* "Yes, I am having a baby…I'm a bit confused as to what this has to do with anything."

"Eva, it has everything to do with working here. Although we will be using mostly plant-based materials for our products, you may have to eventually go to the Tech House and there will be radiation and sometimes-harmful chemicals. Especially when we have to dissect other brands and our competitor's products." She paused as if trying to find the right words. "I'm not saying you should quit, I think in a few more years you will be a valuable asset to the company. So just, think about things. And of course, you will need a doctor's write-off that will enable you to work in those conditions." Knowing it was the end of that conversation, Eva rose and left the office.

Chapter Thirty-Seven:

Evangeline

Eva was finally home when she had exactly two hours to dress and get herself ready for the engagement party. She called and made an appointment with her OB/GYN for the following Monday. Now that it was taken care of she went to the kitchen and made herself some hot tea. Sue was at the beauty salon getting her hair and make-up done. Her phone rang. She looked at the screen and it was an unfamiliar number.

"Hello."

"Eva its Linnie I'm outside could you open the door please it's raining like hell out her." *Linnie?* What could she possibly want? Granted she was the Aunt of the baby, if Braxton signs over his rights, then she wouldn't be. Eva figured Linnie, like Braxton, did not want anything to do with the baby. She put her tea down and walked to the door to open it. It was pouring rain outside and the clouds were getting darker. She just hoped there was not going to be a thunderstorm. She had talked to her therapist and told her of her pregnancy. She advised her not to take the Ambien and to try tea before she slept.

"Come in Linnie." Linnie shrugged off her raincoat while wearing the clothes she planned on for the engagement party.

"Eva, I'm just going to cut to the chase."

OK, so much for small talk.

"OK, go ahead." Eva went to retrieve her tea, taking slow sips of the hot liquid.

"You really fucked my brother up, and I don't appreciate it at all. He is the only person I have in this world. Why the hell would you sleep with him and know that you were pregnant with some other man baby?" Her face was flushed and her hair a little damp from the rain. Eva sat her cup on the counter, recalling all his messages and the look of what she thought was hurt was disgust.

How did he come to that conclusion or was that just his

sister?

"Linnie is that what he told you?" She rolled her

eyes.

"Look Eva I'm not judging I know you and Brax

were never officially together, so I understand, but you

need to know. I have never seen him like this before." She

took Eva's hand in hers.

"For whatever reason he loves you, I can tell, and

he is hurt, he feels betrayed…Do you know that you are the

only woman to ever come to his home? Spent the night?

You have Brax doing crazy things and he is hurt and alone

now. I cannot even get through to him. He has had his head

in the bottle for the last two days."

Eva laughed.

"This is funny to you!" Linnie Spat. Stopping she

started to cry again.

"No of course it is not funny. Although your brother is quite dumb for a man they call a genius."

"I'm not following."

"Linnie, I don't have a clue why he thought I was having sex was someone else. That is almost as ridiculous as the fact that he took my virginity and within ten seconds I was pregnant. Not literally of course but yes…Your brother is the father of my baby not some other man."

"So you didn't sleep with anyone else." Eva shook her head and Linnie let out a breath that she was holding. Then she became tense.

"Linnie what is it?"

"Um…I went to the office before I came here and that's when he told me that you were pregnant by someone else. As I was leaving out Michelle was coming in."

Eva did not say anything she was not going to let him think the worst of her, and she damn sure was not letting that blonde Barbie or that fossil of a woman take him from her.

She took the keys to her old Ford Fusion. She bought but rarely drove because of gas prices and New York's traffic. She ran through the rain driving fast, she needed to get to him before he slept with Michelle. If he did then she could not go back to him.

How could he think so little of her? She tried to call him, but his phone was just ringing. She left a message.

Braxton its Angel…I know what you think but it is not true, how could you think that of me. Braxton, I am sorry I left but I did not want to choose between you and our child. I love you.

That was the first time that she said that aloud it gave her more urgency because she needed to tell him to his face. She did not bother to park her car in the employees parking garage. She parked out front in a no parking zone. She ran to the elevator pushing up to the twentieth floor. It was not too late, she hoped. She walked fast to his office and stopped short. When she heard a woman's giggle that she knew to be Michelle's, Eva turned the doorknob, but nothing could have prepared her for what she saw.

Michelle was sprawled in a mini loveseat in his office, his face buried at her breast, his hands slowly sliding up her thighs. When she must have made a noise because Braxton's head shot up. She backed up into the door as Michelle made no move to shield her naked breast. Her voice, in a choked whisper, tears slowly cascading down her face.

"I'm sorry." Eva whispered her voice full or regret, sorrow and anguish. She turned and ran back to the elevator pushing the button repeatedly as if it would make it move faster. When the door opened, she stepped inside, and Braxton was there. His hair was rumpled. His tie slightly skewed to the side. He looked like he had been drinking.

He held the elevator doors open with his hands braced on both sides.

"Angel why are you here?" She could not speak her mind going back to the nasty scene that would be burned in her mind forever.

Had he fucked her already?

She would not leave without him knowing that he too made a mistake. She held her chin up high as she spoke the words that she thought was going to save them not knowing they would be the last heartfelt words she would speak to him.

"I came here because your sister came to see me. She said you told her I was sleeping with you and some other guy. I have never been with another man in my life and I do not understand how you came to that conclusion. You were the only man I have ever been with. And right now, I can see that was the second mistake I made."

She was breathing fast, a cramp growing in her abdomen. She would tell him everything before she really walked out of his life.

"Second mistake?"

"Yes, and the first was falling in love with a person like you. You claim you are hurt! I see the hurt in your eyes as you were seconds from fucking that old bitch!" She cried, holding back sobs and screams that she knew she was going to let out sooner rather than later.

"Braxton from the bottom of my heart I hope that you rot in hell." There she said it.

"Angel are you saying…" A lonely tear meandered down his face. Not from pain but the realization that he messed up again.

"Yes, Braxton I am saying you are the father of this baby…no you are the sperm donor. I never want to see you again. And I QUIT!" She shoved him against his chest, never leaving her as the elevator doors closed between them, shutting him out of her life forever.

As soon as the elevator stopped in the lobby, she bolted to her car. Driving not caring where she drove to just as long as it was far away. Lightning flashed through the sky followed by a blast of thunder. She was shaking between her tears and the rain her vision was blurred. She cried thinking about the moment her life changed when Braxton brought her home from the mugging. Traffic was clear so she wove her car around the sprinkle of cars on the road.

It was too late for her to react as she sped directly into the line of a train. Pressing her breaks repeatedly the car wouldn't slow. Unable to jerk her car around she closed her eyes knowing this was it. The train collided with her little car, tumbling it over and over until it landed upside down. She tasted blood, her body in excruciating pain, she saw flashing lights. She heard someone screaming for help.

Braxton is that you? Did you come after me? I'm here and I'm in pain. Help me and your son. She closed her eyes to savor the memories of Braxton's touch and his kisses. The way his eyes turned from that sexy silver to the smoky grey. If only she could turn back time to when they were happy, before she left him not believing in him, in them. Everything was fading, she held on, wishing her last memories to be of the two of them walking along the beach with a honey-kissed silver-eyed boy with dark locks of hair. She smiled at that memory and then everything went blank.

Epilogue

Braxton wanted to shove his fist into the wall. How could he have been delusional to think that Angel would be anything but his imperfect perfection? Michelle came behind him tugging at his waistband.

"Braxton darling just forget about her. We have some unfinished business to take care of." He pushed her hands away from his person, steam rising from his body.

"Michelle that would be the second worst mistake that I made in the last seventy-two hours." Braxton looked up and down disgusted at what he was doing.

"I do believe you can show yourself out there is something I have to do." He darted to the parking garage on his motorcycle. The rain was getting heavier as he rammed his gears and rode as fast as he could. He could see Angel's car thirty feet away as she wove in and out of the moving cars on the road. It wasn't until he was twenty feet away that he noticed a train coming and Angel's car being hit and rolling until it was upside down and smoke coming out the hood. He immediately dialed 911. His bike screeched to a halt. His world was going in a downward spiral with no hopes of reaching an end, He screamed for help as the bystanders came to look at the scene. Braxton came to the driver's side afraid to touch her, fearing he would make things worse. He laid his head down on broken glass. The shards cutting against his skin. He was absent pain. Just his heart being torn as he sees Angel's mangled body.

"Angel, stay with me please. Angel…Angel…do not close your eyes." He took his jacket off and laid it under her head. His heart started to beat frantically as he heard the sirens. After what seemed like hours he felt someone pull him up.

"Sir, do you know this person?" He said the first thing that came to his mind.

"Yes, she is my fiancé, and she is pregnant, please help them." The officer pulled him towards the ambulance.

"We will do everything we can for her, I just need you to stay calm and relax." Braxton was numb. He looked as they pulled her broken bloody figure from the car. He heard paramedics say she had no pulse. For the first time in twenty-one years. Tears flowed freely from his face.

In the background amid all the chaos were two people. A pair of blue eyes and a woman with fiery red hair stood behind the tape hiding their grins with a mask of an umbrella. Triumphant.

A Note from the Author:

Hi Everyone! I hope you enjoyed reading about Evangeline and Braxton as much as I had the pleasure of bringing their characters to life. I know major cliffhanger right…LOL! What can I say, I am a sucker for wanting more and not wanting an ending…YET! I plan to publish book II in the very near future. Perhaps winter 2021/2022. In addition to this story I am writing another "Cyn Like Sin". I hope we all can connect somewhere on the web. I look forward to hearing your thoughts, critiques and reviews.

Stay Connected:

Instagram: @zaharared

Twitter: @red_zahara

Facebook: Zahara Red

Tiktok: @zaharared

Email me: zaharaa.red@gmail.com

Made in the USA
Coppell, TX
14 August 2021

60503311R00135